Kate Fortune's Journal Entry

I couldn't be happier about Kelly and Mac's wedding! Thank goodness Mac knows the meaning of family honor and doing the right thing, especially since Kelly Sinclair has always been more like a daughter to me than an employee. Mac knows how worried I've been about Kelly once I learned how his brother Chad took advantage of her trusting innocence and ran off, leaving her pregnant and unwed! I'm just so proud of the way Mac's taken charge of this awful situation, and I know he's going to make Kelly a wonderful husband.

It's been such fun helping these two dears plan their wedding. Oh, I know they're not in love now! But I think Kelly's about to show Mac exactly what's missing in his life.... And I can hardly wait to see what this new year holds for them and the rest of my precious family!

Dear Reader,

Welcome to a new year with Silhouette Desire! We begin the year in celebration—it's the 10th Anniversary of MAN OF THE MONTH! And kicking off the festivities is the incomparable Diana Palmer, with January's irresistible hero, Simon Hart, in *Beloved*.

Also launching this month is Desire's series FORTUNE'S CHILDREN: THE BRIDES. So many of you wrote to us that you loved Silhouette's series FORTUNE'S CHILDREN— now here's a whole new branch of the family! Award-winning author Jennifer Greene inaugurates this series with *The Honor Bound Groom*.

Popular Anne Marie Winston begins BUTLER COUNTY BRIDES, a new miniseries about three small-town friends who find true love, with *The Baby Consultant*. Sara Orwig offers us a marriage of convenience in *The Cowboy's Seductive Proposal*. Next, experience love on a ranch in *Hart's Baby* by Christy Lockhart. And opposites attract in *The Scandalous Heiress* by Kathryn Taylor.

So, indulge yourself in 1999 with Silhouette Desire— powerful, provocative and passionate love stories that speak to today's multifaceted woman. Each month we offer you six compelling romances to meet your many moods, with heroines you'll care about and heroes to die for. Silhouette Desire is everything *you* desire in a romance novel.

Enjoy!

Joan Marlow Golan
Senior Editor, Silhouette Desire

Please address questions and book requests to:
Silhouette Reader Service
U.S.: 3010 Walden Ave., P.O. Box 1325, Buffalo, NY 14269
Canadian: P.O. Box 609, Fort Erie, Ont. L2A 5X3

THE
HONOR
BOUND
GROOM

JENNIFER
GREENE

SILHOUETTE *Desire*

Published by Silhouette Books

America's Publisher of Contemporary Romance

Special thanks and acknowledgment are given to
Jennifer Greene for her contribution to the
Fortune's Children miniseries.

 SILHOUETTE BOOKS

SISBN 0-373-76190-2

THE HONOR BOUND GROOM

Copyright © 1999 by Harlequin Books S.A.

JENNIFER GREENE

lives near Lake Michigan with her husband and two children. Before writing full-time, she worked as a teacher and a personnel manager. Michigan State University honored her as an "outstanding woman graduate" for her work with women on campus.

Ms. Greene has written more than fifty category romances, for which she has won numerous awards, including three RITA Awards from the Romance Writers of America in the Best Short Contemporary Books category, and she entered RWA's Hall of Fame in 1998. She is also the recipient of a Career Achievement award from *Romantic Times Magazine*.

F RTUNE'S
Children

Meet the Fortunes—three generations of a family with a legacy of wealth, influence and power. As they gather for a host of weddings, shocking family secrets are revealed...and passionate new romances are ignited.

KELLY SINCLAIR: This sweet, single woman trusted the wrong man, but she's determined to do anything to protect the littlest Fortune—even if it means marrying the baby's uncle!

MAC FORTUNE: The brooding CEO thought he knew all about being responsible and acting honorably when he proposed a marriage-in-name-only to pregnant Kelly Sinclair. Until she and precious Annie moved into his home, and suddenly, keeping them at arm's length became physically—and emotionally—impossible....

ANNIE FORTUNE: This adorable baby may be the youngest Fortune, but she's a heartbreaker-in-waiting for the next generation.

KATE FORTUNE: She's just celebrated her eightieth birthday, but the family matriarch is still going strong, rejuvenated by all the lovely newcomers to the Fortune family!

One

The wedding was a mistake. Getting married had seemed an outstanding idea to Kelly Sinclair two weeks ago, last week and even when she'd woken up this morning. But that was then and this was now. At this precise moment, Kelly realized—with a flash of brilliant clarity—that she'd have to be bonkers to go through with this.

The creamy gardenias clutched in her hands started trembling and wouldn't quit. Anxiety sloshed in her stomach in sick, dread-filled waves. Maybe most brides suffered some nerves on their wedding day, but the average, normal bride wasn't seven months pregnant. She not only felt scared, but she also felt ugly, fat and scared—a lethal combination. To add insult to injury, her pregnant condition made a swift escape an especially challenging problem. Her fastest speed was a waddle. A duck could probably beat her in a sprint.

She tested her memory for any time in her life when she might have been this petrified—but no. There was nothing to compare to this level of terror. At twenty-seven, Kelly had certainly been hurt before. She'd been frightened before. But she'd never been in a situation where she felt this hopelessly, helplessly trapped. Panic was swimming in her pulse.

The door to the bathroom whooshed open. Kate Fortune, the seventy-year-old matriarch of the Fortune Cosmetics empire, poked her head in and then marched straight toward the bride. With slim, competent hands, she gently tugged the pearl-seed veil resting on Kelly's blond curls a little down to the left. "Everyone's seated. I told them to start the wedding march in two minutes. And I thought you might need some last-minute help, but I can see you're all ready. And you look absolutely breathtaking, sweetheart."

Kelly met the older woman's eyes in the vanity mirror. "I look like a watermelon stuck on a toothpick."

"You sure do—and I'm so jealous. There's nothing like a pregnancy to give a woman a special radiance, and you've got it in spades." Just as Kate stepped back to give her one last critical look-over, the door whooshed open again.

Mollie Shaw charged in with a brilliant smile, her long red hair swinging halfway down her back. "There's our bride! I figured you'd be having some last-minute jitters and wanted to tell you that everything's ready, nothing to worry about. Hi, Ms. Fortune—man, do I love that smoky blue dress. It's so elegant, looks wonderful on you. And, Kel, you couldn't possibly be more gorgeous...."

Mollie gently tugged Kelly's veil just a little down on the right. "...and now you're perfect. The music's going to start in just a minute or so. Remember what I told you about taking three deep breaths?"

"Yes."

"Okay, I'm going back out—but you know I'll be around to help during the reception. Everything's going to be fine, sweetie. Trust me."

Nothing was going to be fine. But Mollie had already charged back out the door before Kelly could get a word in—much less find the courage to announce her escape plans and that the whole deal was off.

"That girl's face is so familiar," Kate said absently.

The comment confused Kelly enough to distract her—at least for a second. "Well, sure she's familiar—you know Mollie, Kate—"

"Yes, and she's been a godsend. Lucky for all of us that your friend was already in the wedding planner business. As young as she is, she's really a dynamo. I don't know how we could have put all this together in two short weeks without her. It's not that. It's just that her red hair and green eyes are so distinctive, and every time I see her face I think I should recognize her from somewhere else, but I just can't place it. Well...it certainly doesn't matter now. Especially when we've only got a few more seconds, and there's something I really want to tell you."

Kate fixed the veil one more time. Her way. If she noticed the bride's crepe white pallor or the frantic alarm in her eyes, she never let on. "Kelly...I'm so honored that you're letting me be the one to give you away. I'm sorry your mom isn't still alive to be part of this—she'd be so proud. But I want you to know, I couldn't care more if you were my own daughter."

Well, spit. Her conscience was already suffering from muck-deep guilt, and Kate's words only made her feel worse. She *had* to tell Kate that her mind was made up; the wedding was off—there was no way she could possibly go through with it. But somehow she couldn't get the words said.

Kate had done so much for her. Four years ago when Kate had plucked her from the pool of clerks and given her the job as her personal social secretary, Kelly's whole life had irrevocably changed. Most people found her boss to be irascible and ruthless and domineering. She was all those things—even to her family—but never to Kelly. Their working relationship had long turned personal. Kate was the one who had picked out the cream satin wedding dress with the pearl-studded collar and cuffs. The simple style with the subtly draping pleats almost hid her beached-whale-size tummy, and heaven knew it was the most glamorous, gorgeous dress she'd ever owned. And it wasn't just the blasted dress. Kate had paid for the wedding, the clothes, everything, even made all the arrangements to have the ceremony at the Fortune company headquarters—probably the one place on earth where they could control security and be completely protected from the media.

Kate had private reasons for wanting this wedding to happen. Kelly realized that, but it didn't make her debt of gratitude any less. She'd still been treated like a daughter. "Kate, I had no idea that you were going to go to so much trouble and expense—"

"Nonsense. Your friend Mollie did all the legwork. I just helped with a bit of the organizing. It was a joy to arrange, no trouble at all."

Kelly knew better. She'd never asked for any of it, but every detail from the out-of-season gardenias to the designer dress to the champagne reception was a measure of how much trouble her boss had gone to. She also hadn't realized how much Mollie and Kate had conspired behind her back until everything was already done. Another layer of guilt troweled on her conscience. They'd both been so wonderful to her. She really didn't want to show her ingratitude by hightailing it for the front door at a wallowing gallop, but there was only one word screaming in her mind. Escape.

Abruptly she heard the first strains of the wedding march. Adrenaline bolted through her bloodstream, and a lump clogged her throat bigger than the Rock of Gibraltar. She couldn't go through with this. She just couldn't.

"There now." Kate also heard the music and firmly, securely, tucked her arm in hers. "Here we go...just think calm and put a smile on, and don't worry about a thing. Everything's going to work out.''

Nothing was going to work out, but it seemed like only a millisecond passed before Kate had effectively herded her the few steps across the hall to the long, tall set of double mahogany doors. She could see Sterling, Kate's husband, waiting just inside. And Renee Riley, her maid of honor, shot her a wink, before starting her walk-down-the-aisle thing. Kate's grip never loosened when Kelly cast a swift, frantic glance over her shoulder.

The exit wasn't visible from here, but she glimpsed the lobby windows. Outside, holiday decorations still wreathed the streetlights and snow was clearly pelting down in a stinging fury. Not untypical of a New Year's Eve in Minnesota, the winter wind was howling like a banshee. The snowstorm had been building momentum since midafternoon, as if the weather gods had figured out her state of mind and were sending an omen. This was a bad idea. A disastrous idea.

In fact, she made a prompt New Year's resolution to never again get married for as long as she lived.

But in those teensy milliseconds, Kate had propelled her to the middle of those open doors, in full view of the guests. The place wasn't recognizable as a conference room. In one sweeping glance, Kelly saw the red velvet carpet, the satin ribbons draping the chairs, the dais at the front of the room transformed with pots and sprays of fragrant gardenias and baby's breath and heart-red roses. She also saw the guests all rising in traditional respect for the bride and thought: they weren't gonna like it when she cut and run.

The minister smiled reassuringly at her from the front of the room. She thought: his smile was gonna disappear fast when the bride hiked up her skirts and took a fast powder.

The gathering only seemed crowded because every chair was filled, the room stuffed with people, yet the guests couldn't number much over thirty. She knew every face.

They were either Fortunes or related kin—none of her own family, because she had none...not anymore—but God knew the Fortunes had taken her in as if she were part of their clan. Everyone knew when and how she'd gotten into trouble. Everyone had gone out of their way to stand by her, and their choosing to attend the wedding was another measure of that support.

An already catastrophic situation just kept getting worse. Undoubtedly they were expecting to attend the usual nice, peaceful, happy ceremony. Instead all they were going to get was a mortified bride running helter-skelter into a snow-storm. In cream satin shoes and no coat.

Kate gripped her arm more securely, urging her forward, yet her hold was never really that tight. Kelly knew she could shake free. It was just a matter of picking her moment. This marriage wasn't just a mistake. It was a mistake the size of an earthquake. Maybe she'd have to leave the country under an assumed name to live this down, but she simply couldn't go through with it.

But then this strange thing happened.

It wasn't as if the minister or Kate's grip or the whole sea of faces instantly disappeared...but her gaze suddenly locked on the groom.

Mackenzie Fortune.

Mac.

His shoulders looked beam-broad in the black tux, his height towering, his thick hair darker than charcoal and shot with silver at the sideburns. Black suited him, the same way it would suit a pirate. His angular face was set with strong bones and an elegant mouth and a no-nonsense square chin.

Nobody messed with Mac. The lean, mean build had nothing to do with it. He was a business man, not a pirate dependent on brawn to get his way. She'd never heard him raise his voice, never seen him angry, but he had a way of silencing a whole room when he strode in. Those shrewd, deep-set green eyes could cut through chatter faster than a blade. The life lines bracketing his eyes and mouth reflected an uncompromising nature, a man who loved a challenge and never backed down from a fight. Mac was a hunk, but he was also one intimidatingly scary dude—at least for a woman who was uncomfortable around powerful men.

A year before, Kelly had been wildly, blindly, exuberantly in love. The father of her baby had been an incredibly exciting man. A man she believed in heart and soul. A man she would have done anything for, anytime, anywhere, no questions asked—and unfortunately, had.

Mac wasn't the man she'd been in love with.

He wasn't the father of her baby.

He was just the groom.

But his gaze met hers with the directness of a sharp, clear laser beam as if no one else were in that room but the two of them. He didn't smile—but that look of his immediately affected the panicked beat of her pulse. She was unsure what the dark, fathomless expression in his eyes meant, but that wasn't news. She was unsure of nearly everything about Mac, but she promptly forgave herself for the wild panic attack. Surely it was understandable. Normally a woman would have to be crazy to marry a relative stranger, but nothing about Kelly's life right now was normal. For a few moments there, she'd just selfishly forgotten what mattered—and it wasn't her.

If there was a man on the planet who could protect her baby, it was Mac Fortune.

Nothing else mattered to her or even came close.

She took a breath for courage, plastered on a smile and walked up the aisle to her groom.

At thirty-eight, Mac had no belief in magic, but he'd always felt a certain kinship with Houdini. He understood how much hard work it took to become an accomplished escape artist. For Mac, it had taken ceaseless determination and unfaltering resolve and downright dedication to escape marriage all these years—particularly when the family never stopped hounding him to tie the knot. More than a few women had chased him—most were more interested in a key to the Fortune money than in him personally, but that hadn't bothered Mac. He had always respected both greed and ambition. He'd enjoyed being chased. Hell, he enjoyed women. He just happened to have a violent allergy to marriage.

Kelly had almost reached the edge of the red velvet carpet when Mac saw her stumble. She didn't trip, but he could see the stress swimming in her eyes. Without hesitation, he swiftly stepped forward and grabbed her hand. The minister's brow furrowed in a repressive little frown, silently letting Mac know that he'd broken with protocol in this shindig. Apparently the groom wasn't supposed to put his mitts on the bride at this point in the proceedings. Reaching out to grab her wasn't in the program.

Tough. Kelly looked fragile enough to keel over. Ghosts had more color. And judging from the sweat dampening his bride's shaky palm, she was even less thrilled by this marriage than he was. The humorous thought crossed his mind that at least they had a couple of things in common. Neither wanted this wedding.

And neither had seen any way out of it.

"Dearly beloved," the minister began in a sonorous drone.

Mac tuned out. Keeping his fingers curled in hers, he mentally calculated how soon they could escape this circus. The ceremony couldn't take more than fifteen minutes? And then they were on the hook to stick around for the champagne feast Kate had put together. But the blizzard forecast would surely cut this short for everyone. In less than two hours, with any luck, they could be driving home—long before the clock struck midnight and brought in the new year.

He felt eyes on his back. Watching him, studying him.

At any wedding, the groom and bride were obviously the focus of attention, but Mac was well aware these circumstances were different. As vice president of Finance for the Fortune Corporation for almost a decade, his job had often been to bail the business—or the family—out of trouble. The clan was long on love and loyalty, but big money still made for big problems and big disagreements as well. If there was a problem that could cause embarrassment, someone had to make the boo-boo disappear. When everyone else was freaked out and wringing their hands, Mac had a long history for taking charge and doing what had to be done.

This time, though, they weren't so sure of him.

He'd announced two weeks ago that he was going to marry her. It was the first time he'd ever seen the family stunned to silence. Part of that silence was relief—the problem of Kelly was no secret, but no one could agree on solutions. Even for a family who would lie, cheat and steal for each other—and sometimes, unfortunately, took loyalty just that far—nobody had considered that marriage was an optional solution for this crisis, much less for Mac. They knew about his allergy. They couldn't believe he meant it. They still weren't dead positive he'd go through with it.

Kelly's hand suddenly squeezed his. He glanced down. For an instant he caught the tiniest hint of humor in her eyes. "The ring," the minister prompted. From the high-pitched crack in Reverend Lowry's voice, Mac suspected he'd missed his cue at least once.

His cousin Garrett Fortune, thankfully, was prepared to do the best-man job, and quickly palmed him the ring. Mac reached for Kelly's left hand. The slim gold band was almost microscopic—hardly appropriate for a Fortune bride. But he'd offered Kelly any size carat rock she wanted, and she'd balked. She wanted no jewels and particularly no stones with a Fortune heritage—probably because it was

Fortune money that had heaped this whole mess on her head.

Yet as he struggled to fit on the ring, he was suddenly aware of her. Distractingly aware. He'd clasped her hand to offer support, but there was nothing intimate in that simple act of kindness. She was so nervous that her slim white hand was trembling like a leaf in a high wind. But her dress rustled against his thigh. And her scent drifted to his nostrils, some perfume that vaguely reminded him of spring daffodils, illusive and sweet. And he saw a silvery pale curl sneaking down behind the veil, escaping a hairpin, coiling on the pale white column of her neck. Mac wasn't sure why his pulse suddenly bucked—possibly because it hit him with the slam of a freight train that he didn't know her. At all.

But the ring stuck on her knuckle, and then he pushed it past.

"With this ring..." The minister said, and then waited.

Kelly nudged him with her foot. "With this ring," Mac repeated loudly and clearly.

"I thee wed..."

She didn't have to nudge him this time. "I thee wed."

"I promise to love, honor and cherish..."

Normally telling lies would have bothered him. But not for this. The integrity of a man was measured in honor— an antiquated value that Mac happened to believe was the judge of a man's life. But the truth of this moment was between him and Kelly, and a bunch of words said in public had nothing to do with that.

Still, the fibs obviously didn't come so easily for her. When it was her turn to put a ring on his finger, she fumbled and flustered and almost dropped it. "With this ring," she started reciting.

Her voice barely managed the volume of a whisper. She had trouble pushing the ring onto his finger, and Mac could sense how uneasy she was about touching him. She couldn't or wouldn't meet his eyes when it was done, but again they were close. He could see the sweep of velvet-soft eyelashes shading her cheeks, the faint spray of freckles across the bridge of her nose.

God, she was young. It wasn't the age difference between thirty-eight and twenty-seven that separated them half so much as the light-years of experience. In spite of her protruding tummy being obvious proof to the contrary, she still had a look of innocence. There were those freckles. And those shy, sky-soft blue eyes. And that silky fine hair that normally bounced on her shoulders and never looked brushed. She was a half foot shorter than him—squirt size—and her oval face was set with delicate, fine features, but there was nothing elegant or delicate about the way she ran around the company. Hell, he'd heard her giggling in Kate's office more than once, and she chased around with this radiant, exuberance zest for life that made the sun seem low-voltage by comparison. She was a grown-up, intelligent woman, and she handled a bundle of responsibilities for Kate, but nothing had ever sobered that so-young cheeky smile of hers. Until Chad took off and left her.

Mac mentally damned his younger brother—not for the first time in the last few months. Chad could charm a woman into bed faster than a bee could smell honey. He also had a gift for disappearing from sight whenever there was music to face. Truth to tell, Chad hadn't known about the pregnancy when he disappeared this time, but he'd paid his way out of a paternity suit before. Maybe if Mac had listened earlier to gossip, he'd have heard about Chad giving Kelly a rush and done something about it—but maybe not. Over the years, he'd tried counseling, tried yelling, tried bailing Chad out of countless scrapes, but nothing seemed to root a sense of responsibility or honor in his younger brother. Initially Mad had tried to locate him when the situation took a serious nose dive, but Chad had cut and run for parts unknown—par for his course. Eventually, he was findable. With enough money, anyone was findable. But the problem of Kelly required immediate action, and Mac had lost all faith that his brother would step up to the plate even if he were in the ball park.

Kelly suddenly raised her eyes and looked at him. She was obviously trying to communicate something, but damned if he could read the message in her eyes. Hell, for a minute he couldn't even think.

His mind spun back two weeks ago—to the night when she'd been attacked in the parking lot on the way to her car. He'd known she was pregnant long before then. He'd known she was wildly in love with his brother, and that Chad was unquestionably responsible for the pregnancy. And those factors added up to a problem that involved family—but not a problem that directly affected him until that night.

She'd stayed late, finishing up something for Kate—so late the parking lot had been pitch-dark and deserted, so late there were only a handful of people in the whole building when she'd escaped her attacker and raced inside looking for help.

Mac just happened to be the first body she saw, and those moments were still carved in his memory with indelible black ink. He'd known Kelly for years, but their contact had only been peripheral; she was either running around, doing something for Kate or with Kate. They had few reasons to directly cross paths. Recently he'd tried to catch a closer look at her because the family was having such a royal cow about Chad and the pregnancy, but that was tough to do—invariably she skittered around him or ducked from sight. Mac couldn't do his job, not well, and fuss whether he was winning popularity contests. He was so used to people being uncomfortable around him that Kelly's response didn't bother him one way or the other. That night, though, Mac doubted that Kelly knew or cared who he was. He could have been saint or sinner, God or the janitor—it wouldn't have made a lick of difference to Kelly.

She came chasing through the glass doors of the lobby, running hell-bent for leather. There was a receptionist/guard at the front desk, but she didn't even seem to see him. Her hair was all tumbled, no coat even though it was subzero outside; her cheek was scraped, a stocking ripped and her right knee bloody. She was crying and hiccuping and damn near hysterical and she hurled straight for the nearest body with the ballast of a missile. She'd almost knocked him over—and Mac was no powder puff.

Her missing coat was how she'd escaped the son of a bitch. There had been some point in the struggle when the SOB had grabbed her and only got a handful of coat, which enabled her to shimmy loose from the garment and run. Right then, it was tough to get even that much out of her, because she had no interest whatsoever in talking about her attacker. She'd fallen, and was petrified something had happened to her baby.

Faster than ten minutes, Mac had both the cops and a doctor there. He'd left her with a woman employee and the doctor, but the whole time he was with the police, Mac could feel the tension coiling in his stomach. As he could have guessed, the cops could find no clues to the identity or motivation of her assailant. It could have been a garden-variety purse snatcher; it could have been some nut-case psychopath. But Kelly's involvement with Chad had been spread in the press early on in their relationship, simply because anything the Fortunes did was news. And that meant, unfortunately, that it was public knowledge that she was carrying a Fortune child.

There had been kidnappings in the family before. Kidnappings, threats, blackmail attempts; thieves—hell, there was no limit to the criminal element hot to prey on a family with money like his.

Later that evening, he'd taken Kelly to her home, sat

with her until she calmed down, poured her a glass of milk and himself a bourbon—it was the only alcohol drink she had in her apartment—and proposed marriage. It was the first time he'd heard her even try to laugh that evening. And when she realized he was serious, she got another case of hiccups.

Marrying a woman because she was pregnant would never necessarily have aroused Mac's sense of honor. Hell, you couldn't solve one disaster by compounding it with another. But that happened to be his nephew growing in her womb. A Fortune child. And whether she'd volunteered for the problems that came with being a Fortune when she fell for his scoundrel of a brother, there was no escaping them now. The baby had the best chance of being protected from within the family circle—the Fortune name, the Fortune power, the Fortune protection. She had the chance to give the baby his birthright as well as insure the child's future. Mac wasn't closing any doors to choices down the pike—for her, or for him. Hell, he knew she was in love with his brother—but love had nothing to do with this problem and couldn't solve it. Right then the only choice he saw to effectively protect the child was a legal alliance between them.

She'd said yes that night—Mac knew—because she'd been scared. Not just scared from the attack itself, but stunned-scared from realizing that attack could be just the tip of an iceberg. Maybe she'd just fallen in love with a man, but her making love with a Fortune had volunteered her for a ton of repercussions she'd never expected.

And belatedly, Mac suddenly recognized that Kelly looked scared right now. Not terrorized or anything that traumatic, but one of the few things—in fact, damn near the only thing—Mac knew about his bride was how she responded when she was shook up. Her face was tilted up to his, so it wasn't as if she was trying to hide her expression from him. Two dots of fire-engine red dotted her cheeks. The pulse in her throat was beating like a manic clock. Her soft blue eyes were shooting him an increasingly urgent message. Hell, she was probably going to start hiccuping any second.

With a frown, he glanced at the minister. Reverend Lowry was as red-faced as Kelly. The instant he caught the groom's eyes, he repeated loudly, "I now pronounce you man and wife. You may kiss the bride. *Now,* Mac."

Sheesh. Mac could have kicked himself. This was no time to be woolgathering, and more to the point, one short buss for his bride and the two of them were done with this blasted ordeal and closer to being out of there.

He pushed up the fragile, lacy veil to get the nuisance thing out of the way and bent down. For some God-unknown reason, Kelly's eyes flashed an even more frantic message than before. He couldn't imagine what she was worried about. This was just a kiss. A traditional gesture. It wasn't going to take a quarter of a second. Surely she knew she had nothing to fear from him.

And then he kissed her.

The kiss was fast. Faster than a man could suck in a lungful of oxygen—hell, his bride had been a stronger brick through the ceremony than he had. Mac owed her a thankyou. He owed her a promise that she had nothing to fear from him, ever. And when his lips touched down, there was nothing on his mind but a quick, impersonal kiss that shared a mutual desire to get this over with.

But in that blink of time, something went haywire. He couldn't explain it. It was just…her lips were warmer than a summer sun, and soft. Soft like spring, like the stroke of a restless silky breeze. She tasted young and sweet and vibrant, and it seemed like a thousand years since Mac had felt that way. He was a grown man. He'd put aside his boyhood idealism a century ago, but he suddenly remembered that time in his life when he'd been young, so stupid—young, back when love was everything and life offered a nonstop excitement of possibilities. Until that second, he hadn't remembered that huge, yearning, alluring hunger to love in years. He couldn't fathom why a quarter-second kiss from Kelly could possibly have invoked it.

But when he swiftly lifted his head, two dots of color heated his cheeks. And the pulse in his throat was beating like an out-of-control battery.

Two

"How much farther?"

"About five miles." Mac scratched his chin. "About a quarter mile less than the last time you asked me. Is there a problem?"

Now there was a hysterically funny question, Kelly thought dryly. She was freshly married to a stranger. The kiss that sealed their vows had shaken her socks off. The snowstorm had escalated to a mean-cold, wind-howling blizzard, with snow slooshing down so hard that even Mac's elegant Mercedes's windshield wipers could barely keep up. They'd turned off the highway a while back, and she hadn't seen a single car on the road since, much less buildings or lights or any sign of civilized rescue potential if they got stranded—assuming they found anything open this late on a New Year's Eve.

Offhand, yeah, she thought they had a few problems. Yet all those details seemed itsy bitsy compared to the serious problem troubling Kelly at the moment. "How long does it usually take you to drive home from the Fortune head-quarters?''

"Fifteen minutes, twenty max. But it's pretty hard to move faster than a crawl pace with this snow.''

"I know, Mac. I didn't mean to sound impatient.''

"You're not cold, are you? Because I could turn up the heat—''

"No, I'm fine." He'd already cranked up the heater and defroster to full blast. She couldn't be warmer if she were curled up in front of an oven.

"If you're tired, you can put the seat back—''

His concern touched her, but the subject of exhaustion again teased her sense of irony. If anything in life were normal, she'd be snoozing right now. From the beginning of the pregnancy, she'd been prone to nap at the drop of a hat. And after all the stress of the wedding and reception, technically she should be as comatose as a zombie. But that kiss from Mac had shaken her whole equilibrium.

She knew he'd meant nothing by it. She knew she was imagining a potent, sizzling connection that had never happened. It was just hormones again. Kelly had had seven months to discover that pregnancy made a woman emotionally goofy. Impatiently she twisted in her seat. "I'm fine, not the least tired. And the car couldn't be more comfortable,'' she assured him.

Mac glanced at her again as if unconvinced, but of necessity his gaze zipped swiftly back to the road. She could barely see his face in the pitch-dark car—just a glimpse of his patrician profile and a flash of his dark eyes now and then. There simply wasn't enough light to judge from his expression what he might be thinking—about the wedding or the weather or anything else. From the tone of his voice, though, Kelly understood he was deliberately trying to sound calm and quietly reassuring. "If you're worried about the weather, try to take it easy. I've lived here all my life, which means I've driven in a hundred blizzards.

This one has the makings of a doozy—I think we could be socked in for a couple of days—but we'll be under cover before the worst of it hits. The roads are rough, but the problem is snow, not ice. Trust me, we're not going to have any trouble making it home."

"That's good to hear."

But when Mac caught her shifting in her seat again, he seemed to think his previous reassurances hadn't been enough. "Kelly…this whole day's been a pressure cooker, and I know you have to be worried about things. All kinds of things. But we were both honest with each other going into this, and we both want the same thing—to make this work out. I think if we just take it slow and easy, we'll find answers for whatever we need to, one problem at a time. Try and believe it's going to be okay, all right?"

Kelly clipped back a sigh. Mac was not only trying to be considerate and reassuring—he was doing a damn fine job of it. He'd been downright wonderful at the wedding reception, sticking to her side, anticipating problems before they developed. Something had upset her maid of honor, because Renee had turned stark white after a conversation with her father and disappeared almost immediately after. That wouldn't have mattered except that Kelly had counted on Mollie to stay close during the reception, and her closest friend had suddenly left early, too. Both had left without a word, which was so unlike either woman that Kelly had worried…but at the time of the reception, she'd really had her hands full.

Mac's family was unquestionably supportive for this wedding, but there wasn't a shy Fortune in the bunch. Their nosiness came from caring, but she'd felt painfully stranded with the now-you're-family-you-can-tell-me questions. What kind of relationship did she and Mac actually have? How well did she really know Mac? Had either of them heard from Chad? Did Chad even know about this marriage?

Kelly had been heart and soul in love with Chad, but it took sleeping with him to understand that his interest in her was purely seduction, the new conquest. Since then she'd heard rumors that he had taken off with another woman—also some scandal about a paternity suit with another girl. But she'd figured out the measure of Chad long before the first pregnancy test—and her own naiveté in the relationship as well. She'd never have married him, but neither did she want to air the personal details of a painful mistake to anyone, much less publicly. And every time one of those awkward, prying questions surfaced, Mac had shown up like a magician. He never cut anyone off. He was always nice. But no one even tried to misbehave when Mac was around—cripes, even Kate seemed to instinctively defer to him.

Kelly had the humorous impression of a wolf watching out for his lamb—and that rare feeling of being protected had been welcomed. Then. But not now. Now that they were totally alone together, she remembered how much he intimidated her, too. His being a sexy hunk only made her feel more awkward. That velvet-soft baritone of his was curling her toes—but not because of some hormonal response. She just couldn't face bringing up an indelicate problem with the formal, elegant, dauntingly sexy and formidable Financial V.P. for the whole darned Fortune empire. Kelly squirmed in her seat again.

"With road conditions this rough, I really think the seat belt's essential, but they can't have made those things for a pregnant woman. If you're uncomfortable—"

Well, spit. Apparently Mac had perceived there was something wrong and he wasn't going to let it go until she confessed the reason. And it wasn't as if she had a choice about staying silent more than another two seconds, anyway. "Mac, I *am* uncomfortable. But the problem isn't the seat belt or being married or the heat or the weather. It's that I have to go to the bathroom."

"Oh. Um—right now? We really should be home within twenty minutes—"

"I realize this is hard to believe if you've never been seven months pregnant. But twenty minutes from now, I'll be desperate to go all over again. So that won't exactly solve the immediate problem."

"Okay. No reason to be embarrassed. Everything's fine. It just may take me a few minutes to find a gas station. There isn't much open on New Year's Eve, and I'm afraid we're a little removed from—"

"Mac."

"What?"

"Pull over."

"Pull over? Honey, we're in the middle of a blizzard in subzero temperatures—"

She heard the "honey" and felt a wave of sympathy for her poor groom. She'd never seen MacKenzie/Mac Fortune flustered before—even by the threat of a company takeover. "Yeah, well, I should have told you before I got desperate. But I didn't. And I won't survive, Mac. If I had an accident on these incredibly luxurious leather seats, I'd be so mortified I'd never be able to face you again as long as I lived. You'd have my death-by-mortification on your conscience. And we'd have gone through the whole marriage for nothing. We can solve all this if you just pull over, okay? Like...pronto."

Mac pulled over. Pronto. "Do you need, um—"

Before he was reduced to using any more wild endearments, she filled him in. "I've been carrying toilet paper since I was four months pregnant. Believe me, I figured out a while ago that I needed to be prepared."

The winds were gale force, the snow biting like icy teeth, and Kelly thought glumly that this was a hell of an auspicious way to start a marriage. But when she climbed back into the car with wet feet and wet hair and snow sticking to her nose and eyelashes, she caught the hint of a quick-silver grin from Mac.

"I don't think we'd better take you out in too many blizzards for the next couple months," he said dryly.

A startled chuckle escaped Kelly. Holy kamoly. Mac had actually teased her. Who'd a thunk it? And it seemed a crazy thing to be just discovering that her groom had a sense of humor...but she suddenly realized how many things she'd been judging about Mac on limited evidence. She'd assumed he was formal and serious by nature be-cause that's all she'd been exposed to. But their personal conversations over the last couple of weeks had been dead serious because they needed to be. And no, she'd never seen him casually joking around with staff at work before that, but really, how could he? His job was tough and re-quired toughness. If someone had to make an unpopular decision, it always fell on his shoulders.

Maybe authority and toughness came naturally to him, Kelly mused, but the point was that she'd had no oppor-tunity to know any other side of Mac...what he wanted, what he dreamed of, what he was like when the suit and tie came off. Who was there for him when he needed to vent that chestload of endless responsibilities? Heaven knew, she could imagine all kinds of women in his life. But by the farthest stretch of her considerable imagina-tion—none of them remotely resembled the bride he was stuck taking home tonight.

And it seemed only moments later they were there. She barely caught sight of the tall, wrought-iron fence, before Mac was pushing a button that made the double gates elec-tronically swing open. "There are a ton of things I need to show you—like how the security system works. But there's time enough to talk about all that in the morning. I suspect you just want to get settled in and get your feet up. I want you to know, though, that the security system's state of the art. You're safe here, Kel."

"I know." It was the one thing she hadn't worried about in the last two weeks. Since the night she'd been attacked in the parking lot, Kate and the family had cosseted her nonstop, but the security she felt with him was a world apart. She'd feel safe with a lion if Mac were around. It's just the way he was. At this precise moment, though, she suddenly discovered that feeling safe from criminals and feeling safe with her new groom were two entirely different things.

Her pulse started skittering. Once the gates closed behind them, the look of anything civilized disappeared, and the drive seemed to go on forever. Even with the blinding, slashing snow, she could make out certain things. The private road twisted around a creek bed. Pines nestled around one turn, their branches bowed with heavy skirts of snow; a stand of virgin hardwoods stretched in another direction, then a field that rolled and curved and looked as if it was blanketed with whipped cream—there were no footprints in the snow, no sign of man. But up and around a sloping knoll, the house came into view.

The baby suddenly kicked, and Kelly's hand instinctively covered her abdomen. Even with the dim visibility, she recognized the property and house.

Mac had brought her here once, a few days before. Two weeks was an incredibly short time to upend your whole life. He'd insisted she see it to decide if she could live here. Possibly he really meant to give her one last-ditch chance to say no to the whole marriage idea, but truthfully, Kelly never felt as if she had a chance or a choice. The attack had petrified her. She had to protect her baby. Nothing else mattered, but the last two weeks had still felt like a fast-moving train. There hadn't been time to catch her breath, much less figure out what all these monumental changes and decisions really meant.

She still hadn't had that time. But her first look at the

house had touched something inside her. And it did now, even more.

The place was lit up. Snow spiraled in the outside porch lights, and inside lamps shone in the windows like welcoming beacons. Kelly remembered the first time she'd seen Kate Fortune's house. She'd grown up on a struggling single mom's budget, and the opulence of the home base Fortune mansion had her bug-eyed. It just went on and on— the landscaped grounds, objets d'art, priceless rugs, loot and luxuries she'd never seen outside of movies. Kelly remembered thinking God, how easy it would be to develop a lust attack for material possessions. But working with Kate had somehow sabotaged her developing that vice. She'd seen firsthand what a life of privilege was about, and she'd choose a mortgage anytime over having to live in a museum.

But Mac's place was no museum. The house was stone. Two sturdy stories, with gleaming casement windows and gables and arched doorways. Compared to her three-room apartment, it was monster-size—and she hadn't seen all of it—but the place had so much character and personality that it looked like…well, it looked like a home. Smoke chugged out of the chimneys and snow cuddled in the windowsills. Whoever had cleared the walk had left the shovel in the porch overhang. Maybe an ordinary person could live here. Like the kind of person who would forget to put away the shovel. Like her.

She only glimpsed the front for a second, then Mac punched a button and the garage doors opened. A Jeep already took up one parking place—not a fancy Jeep, but one with mud-crusted tires and a little dent in its fanny. It wouldn't particularly have startled her, except that Kelly had never seen Mac dressed less formally than a suit, formally ready for a shot in *GQ*. "The Jeep is yours?"

"Yeah." Mac was already climbing out, the Jeep obviously the last thing on his mind. If he hadn't suddenly rolled his shoulders, she wouldn't have realized that he was whip-tired from the challenging drive—not counting everything else that had happened that day. "Just head inside, Kelly. No one's here—I can't remember if you met Benz and Martha the other day. They live on the far side of the property, do some housekeeping and chores for me, and I've lined them up to come in more often. While I'm at work, I don't want you here alone, especially when you're this far pregnant. But for a few days, I thought you might want to explore the place on your own and not feel like strangers were hovering over you. If you don't remember the layout, that door leads to the kitchen—just settle in wherever you want. I'll follow you in two seconds—I just want to check a few things out here first. The house has a generator if we lose power, and the way this storm's building we could be holed up for a couple of days—oops."

"Oops?" Somehow Kelly didn't think that expression got much of a workout in Mac's normal vocabulary, and suddenly there was that potent quicksilver smile again.

"Yeah, I don't know where my head was. Here I'm rambling on about silly subjects like blizzards, when I should have remembered there are bigger priorities. The bathroom is the first door on the left," he informed her.

She chuckled, and for the craziest moment they shared a smile. A real smile. For an instant she forgot he was a sexy hunk, forgot he was the formidably powerful Mac Fortune, forgot he'd been sucked into protecting the woman his brother got pregnant. For that instant, Mac was just...a man. A man with rumpled dark hair and the shadow of whiskers on his chin and a smile that warmed up those cool green eyes. A man she wanted to know. Not *had* to get to know.

But he had that generator thing he wanted to look at, so she hustled inside. After shedding her coat on a kitchen chair, she kicked off her shoes and peeled promptly for the teal-and-white bathroom she saw off the kitchen.

When she washed her hands, she caught sight of herself in the vanity mirror and immediately considered hiding out in the bathroom—like for the next two weeks. She'd looked worse. She just couldn't remember when. Her fine blond hair was tumbling down, her makeup long gone and the elegant cream satin dress just looked silly over her basketball-size tummy. The bride of Frankenstein surely looked more put-together than this...but objectively Kelly knew that vanity was a pretty silly thing to worry about. Mac had no reason to care what she looked like.

It was just that this was the part of the day she'd dreaded a hundred times more than the ceremony. Facing her new husband. Alone. There was no question or worry about intimacy—even if she weren't seven months pregnant, she couldn't imagine being the kind of woman who would remotely attract Mac. Besides, he'd already broached that lion in its den, and so had she. They had reasons to marry. They had no reason to sleep together—or to feel awkward about that. But the average new bride would undoubtedly be flying into her lover's arms by now...and Kelly didn't know what to do, what to say, or even how to start the whole business of living together.

Well, postponing it wasn't getting the job done—or making it any easier. After running a quick brush through her hair, she charged out. Immediately she noticed that the back door was bolted and the outside lights shut off—and Mac must have hung up her coat because it had disappeared—so he was obviously in the house somewhere.

She padded through the kitchen, trying to remember the downstairs layout. The east side of the house held the kitchen, a long dining room with cushioned window seats and then a library/study kind of room with a fireplace and ceiling-tall bookshelves and a fat, plush, Oriental carpet in a million colors. She half hoped to find Mac there—she'd already identified that room as a great private haven—but no dice.

Across the hall was a polished staircase leading up, and although she didn't remember much about the west side of the house—she didn't have to. She promptly found Mac in the giant living room. And one look from the doorway was enough to make restless nerves prowl through her pulse again.

The room was...stupendous. The ceiling and walls had all been paneled in heart-of-redwood. A stone fireplace arched to the beamed ceiling and was big enough to roast a boar. None of the furnishings were exactly fancy. They were just ultracool guy stuff—a ten-million-button entertainment center, throne-size chairs, two long couches, sturdy antiques with a western flavor, fabrics in a forest green that complemented the rich redwood. The whole darn room was perfect—at least for a guy—except for the pile of battered suitcases and boxes all over the place.

Mac had shed his tux coat and unlatched the buttons at the top of his shirt. Until he saw her, he was hunkered down by the hearth, getting a fire going. Flames were already dancing, licking the kindling, warming the whole room with the tangy scent of pine—but all she could see were her waiflike suitcases cluttering up his elegant room.

He stood up with a smile. "I was wondering if you got lost."

"I'd probably better tell you now—I've got the geographical sense of a deaf bat. I can get lost in a room with one door. You've got a beautiful home, Mac."

"Your home now, too." He motioned to the piled suitcases. "I had your things moved this afternoon so you wouldn't have to be carrying anything on your own—but I couldn't guess on the bigger items like furniture. I thought we could go over to your apartment in a few days? And then you could choose whatever you wanted to bring here—"

"Um, most of my stuff is pretty much early-attic. I don't think anything is exactly going to fit in here too well."

"We'll find room. Or just move some of my things out. For that matter, if you want to redecorate or change something, all you have to do is say. And in the meantime, I didn't mean to dump everything here—or leave it for you to carry. But without asking you first, I didn't know where you wanted to sleep. Do you remember the upstairs?"

"To be honest, no." Actually she remembered the master bedroom—Mac's bedroom—with embarrassing clarity. But she'd been too nervous that day to pay much attention to anything specific about the house.

"Well…upstairs there are five spare bedrooms. I figured you'd want to choose two—one to fix up for the baby and one for you? But I didn't know which ones would suit you without asking. I also thought, you must be exhausted after this long day—maybe you'd just like to pick a bed to sleep in tonight, and save any other decisions until tomorrow or when you feel up to it."

"That sounds fine. I really don't care where I lay my head tonight." Kelly thought this was going like a dream—only too much so. He didn't seem to notice that her suitcases looked like Little Orphan Annie had come to visit. A small tray on the coffee table held two glasses—the one with milk was obviously considerately meant for her. He'd eased into discussing the sleeping arrangements the same way he'd handled the wedding, the drive, everything—Kelly didn't know what she expected, but it was never this level of perception and thoughtfulness. He was taking care of her as if she was precious china, for Pete's sake, when he'd been stuck with this marriage no different than she had.

"We can either go upstairs now and get you settled in…or maybe you'd like to just put your feet up in front of the fire and unwind for a while—"

"Mac." She reached for the glass of milk and gulped down a slug. "Don't you dare say one more kind thing. You're just making me miserable."

"Miserable?" Instantly he quit messing with the fire and surged to his feet. "Hell, why didn't you say something? It is the baby? Are you sick—?"

"No, no, it's not that kind of miserable. I just feel...look, I'm disrupting your whole life. It's one thing to believe we had good reasons for doing this, and another to figure out how to be comfortable together. Everywhere I look you've got this great house all set up for a bachelor, and suddenly you're stuck with a woman who goes in for lace curtains and a pink couch. Somehow we've got to figure out how to talk the same language."

Mac looked confused. "There's no problem, Kelly. If you want lace curtains in here—"

"No. Holy kamoly. No. They'd look awful." The mental picture of frothy curtains against the rich, dark heart-of-redwood almost made her laugh. "I didn't mean I cared about anything like that. I just...would you mind if I asked you some blunt, nosy questions?"

"Of course not. Shoot." He settled in one of the massive forest green chairs and motioned her to take the other.

She considered a straight chair—knowing how hard it was to get in and out of anything these days—but the only straight chair in the room was a mile from Mac. So she sank into the luxuriously fat cushions of the chair across from him and started in. "There are so many things we talked about before. I know you realized how frightened I was the night I was attacked—"

"I know. And I just wish I could change things, Kelly, but I'm afraid criminals tend to prey on a family like the Fortunes."

"I understand that now. But when I fell in love with your brother, I'm afraid I never even thought about his being a Fortune—or how that could affect me or my child." She chugged another gulp of milk. "What I'm trying to say, though, is that your asking me to marry you solved so many things. Just from the angle of protection alone, I've got you behind me, and the Fortune family and those nice, big, tall gates.''

"And your baby will have a name."

She nodded. "Yes. He—or she—will have the last name he's entitled to, and the family relationships that go with that. Securing a future for my baby—Mac, that's everything to me. But we've been through all that, too. All those papers you had me sign. They were all a benefit to me. To my child. You even built an easy out for me into all those legalese papers—''

Mac cocked a black-stockinged foot on the coffee table. From his quizzical expression, he still didn't understand where she was leading this conversation. "The trust we set up for the baby was to secure his future no matter what we choose to do down the road. And we talked about this, Kelly. You're especially vulnerable now, this late in a pregnancy—and right after the baby's born, too. But those circumstances aren't going to be the same, down the pike, and that means you could want to make different choices. We both agreed there's no reason this marriage has to last if it stops working at some point."

Kelly again made a gesture of frustration. "Yes. All that's great. I know all the advantages for me and the baby. But that's just it. It's so one-sided. What on earth is in this arrangement for you?"

Mac's eyebrows arched as if the answer to that question should have been obvious to her. "It was because of my brother that you were put in danger. We may never know if that jerk meant to kidnap you, but there've been kidnappings in the family before. Con artists, thieves, blackmail schemes tried on us. And your relationship with Chad made the society columns often enough to make the public aware that you're pregnant with a Fortune child."

"But it was Chad who put me in that situation. Not you. None of it was your fault, Mac."

"Fault, no. But responsibility is a different thing. We

had a problem on the table that had to be solved—keeping you and the child safe. If fixing that were as simple as hiring security for you, anyone in the family could have done it. It wasn't that simple. You weren't raised in this kind of family. There were risks you had no possible experience to know how to cope with. And money alone was no way to do right for the baby, either." Mac hesitated, and then reached for the glass of scotch from the tray. "Did Chad ever tell you much about our family?"

"Some. Not much. I know your mother died when you were around ten—which had to be terribly hard for you. And I know you're the oldest, that there's a big age gap between you and the twins. I've met Chloe, because she and Chad were so close—"

"Thick as thieves," Mac concurred. "And much as I love them, both of them are hell on wheels—my father just seemed to lose heart after Mom died, let them run wild. But Chad has had the hardest time finding his way. I know his good qualities, and I know you do, too. But growing up, I was so much older that I really felt to blame for not being a stronger influence."

She shook her head. "I understand what you're saying. You felt extra responsible because the baby was Chad's. But this was still your brother's mistake. And mine. Not yours."

"That's my nephew or niece you're carrying. Blood kin. And it could be the closest to a child I'll ever have. Making sure that relationship was a legal tie—"

"Would give you the right to interfere in his upbringing?"

Mac hadn't ducked any blunt questions she'd asked him before, and he didn't evade this one. "To a point. Yes. I wanted a vote in all those million things that come up when you're raising a child—schools, health care, security, the chance to give the kid some coaching and time from the male gender side of the fence—"

"Mac, for heaven's sake, I'd have let you have those things, anyway. And down the road, if we don't agree on issues like that, I assume we'll fight—but no silly legal piece of paper would stop me from telling you if I thought you were overinterfering. But back to what you said a moment ago...why on earth would you think this is your only chance at a child? Why haven't you married?"

She caught a flash of humor in his eyes. "Um...is this where the nosy part of those questions kicks in?"

"Mac, I'm not just asking to be nosy." She struggled to find the right words to explain. "I'm trying to figure out how to make this work for you, not just me. I look around this place and it's a bachelor's paradise. Suddenly you're stuck with a woman who likes clutter and lace and flowers. For that matter, the house I grew up in would probably fit in this living room. I don't know how two people could be more different. And if you never really wanted to be married—"

"All right, I can see where you're headed with this now. And the truth is—I never did plan to marry." Mac scratched his chin. "The whole family's pushed hard for me to tie the knot. I'm not sure I can explain why I haven't. Maybe a wariness just built up over time. Although there are plenty of happy marriages in the family, those aren't the ones I see. If someone's coming to me, it's because there's trouble. Everyone always starts out talking about how much they're in love, but I see what happens when the chips go down, how lives are torn up in the name of love, how the kids are ripped apart when things don't go right. To be honest—"

A log tumbled to the hearth, sending sparks shooting up the chimney. Mac leaned forward as if he were going to promptly go over and tend the fire, but Kelly was afraid she'd never get him talking this way again. "Please. Finish saying whatever was on your mind."

"Well, you might find this hard to believe, but this marriage you and I put together is the first one that ever appealed to me.''

"You have to be kidding. Why?''

"Because I think we've got freedom in this relationship that other couples never have. We can make our own rules. We don't have to do one thing that doesn't work for the two of us. You want to do the whole house in pink—believe me, Kelly, I don't care, go for it. If you don't like anything, all you have to do is say. I'm sure we'll have to compromise on all kinds of things—but neither of us have love or emotions tangled up in this. We can be honest with each other.''

Kelly fell silent, studying her new husband. She could have guessed Mac would value honesty and freedom in a relationship. With his heavy responsibilities, he'd go nuts with a high-maintenance mate—or even a friend—who demanded constant attention. And as always, his expression was self-contained, those wonderful dark eyes of his unreadable. He didn't *seem* lonely. Yet his settling for so little sounded terribly lonely to her. "You don't believe in love, Mac?'' she asked softly.

"Sure. I believe in all kinds of love. Love, loyalty, family, taking care of your own—''

"But not the other kind of love? Between a man and a woman?''

Mac finished the last of his scotch in a gulp, and met her eyes squarely. "I believe the power of hormones can be a hell of a lot of fun—but if one of the things you're worried about is whether I'll be faithful to you, rest your mind. I can't say I'm fond of a celibate lifestyle, but right now…hell, it seems to me we both have our hands full and will for some time. It'd go against my grain to cheat while I was wearing a wedding ring—and whether we're sleeping together doesn't change that. However…''

"However…?''

"However…Chad could come back. Or you could find someone. So could I. That's why we worked out all those prenuptial legal papers, to protect you and the baby no matter what happens to us. There's no such thing as an overnight divorce, Kelly, but we've made it as easy as possible to sever the tie if either of us wants to. As long as we're careful to build this right, we won't have the hurt and anger and emotional baggage that usually goes with a split up. Either we make this work or we've lost nothing. We've still done the right thing for the child. We've still done the right thing to protect you at this moment in time.''

And doing the right thing was obviously a critical thing to her husband, Kelly mused, but there was still a gaping hole in this discussion. He'd asked for nothing from her—except honesty. Maybe Mac didn't want her to have any real place in his life, but she was living here now. There had to be needs she could fill, things she could do for him to at least balance all the things he was doing for her.

But before she could say anything else, she heard a clock chiming in the front hall. One, two, three…abruptly she realized that the clock was going all the way to twelve. In seconds it was going to be the new year.

Mac was diverted by the clock chimes, too, and suddenly stood up with a chuckle. ''It looks like we're both running on empty, but do you have enough milk there to toast the New Year?''

''You bet.'' She leaned forward to grab her milk glass.

''We made it through one incredibly unusual day—thanks to the bride's willingness to kick the groom in the shins when he forgot his lines. Did I remember to say thank you for that?''

''No, but, um…you could pay me back now with a little help.''

His eyebrows lifted. ''What?''

She rolled her eyes with an embarrassed laugh. ''I was trying to stand up for this toast. Only I think I'm stuck. I should have known better than to sit in this chair—the cushions are so deep, and the only thing I can get gracefully out of these days is a straight chair. I feel like an ungainly elephant—''

Before she could even try to scooch forward again, Mac swiftly hooked both her hands and pulled her up. The serious mood was obviously broken, Kelly thought, and they could talk another time. Right now she just figured on toasting the New Year with him and then packing it in. But for just that instant when he helped her up, her protruding tummy grazed against his flat abdomen. And her hands...for some reason he didn't release her hands for another whole millisecond. His grip was warm and strong, his touch sparking an electric rush in her pulse.

She'd felt the same sizzle when he'd kissed her at the wedding. She was positive, then and now, that she was imagining it. He was being kind. He'd frankly brought up sex with her, several times now, with the same ease he'd mentioned having macaroni and cheese for dinner. He thought she was in love with his brother. There wasn't a single rational reason in the universe to think he felt an ounce of attraction for her.

And she didn't. She really didn't.

But for that miniscule second, the muscle in his jaw tightened and some kind of emotion flashed in his eyes. Something bleak and stark. Loneliness. Aloneness. As if he realized—as she did—that a normal bride and groom would never be ending their wedding night this way.

It was just an impulse, while he was already standing as close as a heartbeat, to wrap her arms around him. She didn't want to give her new groom a stroke, and hugs weren't part of their deal. Maybe a hug was presumptuous, but she didn't care. That look of stark loneliness got to her. Everyone needed a plain old affectionate hug sometimes, the warmth of a connection to someone else. If he had a heart attack, then he'd just have to have a heart attack.

He stiffened like a poker when her arms curled around him.

But then he unbent.

Holy cow, did he unbend...

Three

Mac poured another mug of coffee—his fourth that morning—and carried it to the window. The sun hadn't even thought about waking up until past eight. The horizon still had the pink-pearl luster of dawn, making the snowy landscape look as pretty and innocent as a Christmas card—but there'd sure been nothing innocent about the blizzard winds last night. He estimated there were two fresh feet of snow on a level, which wouldn't be that hard to plow out, except that nothing was on a level. Some of the swirling, eddying drifts were taller than him.

With Kel pregnant, he got antsy at the thought of her being cut off from doctors and civilization, even if the city was as shut down as they were. Still, he had a pickup with a blade. He could have their country driveway cleared in a few hours, but for damn sure no one was going anywhere this morning.

Hearing the thump of a distant footfall from upstairs,

Mac immediately spun around. The kitchen was lit up brighter than a hospital surgery. Granted, the teal blue counters and Italian-tile floor were a tad littered, but he'd been working like a dog. Four pans jostled for space on the stove, one for eggs, one for bacon, one for muffins and the last for pancakes. The table was crowded with lined-up boxes of cereal and bowls heaped with apples and oranges and melons—he'd been challenged to find space for silverware, particularly after he'd added pitchers of both orange and cranberry juice.

Mac scratched his chin. Possibly he'd overdone it just a little. Hell, somehow he seemed to have enough food for a battalion of marines, but pregnant women were a completely alien species. He didn't know what Kelly was supposed to eat or what appealed to her, either.

Mac hated being unprepared.

When he heard another footfall, his heart started banging in his chest. Swiftly he shoveled a hand through his hair, checked his jeans zipper, then glanced at his black sweatshirt to make sure there wasn't as much pancake batter on him as there seemed to be on the floor. The sound of footfalls moved to the stairs. He braced as if he were imminently facing a firing squad of Uzi's.

That's exactly what went wrong the night before, Mac figured. He hadn't been braced. He hadn't been prepared. Technically there was nothing wrong with a hug, but he'd just never expected Kelly to suddenly wrap her arms around him. He still had no clue why she'd done it. Maybe every pregnant woman got a wild hair. Maybe she was tired and not thinking. Maybe she needed reassurance. Maybe she'd forgotten she was in love with his brother.

Mac hadn't. Even if he'd tried, the family must have asked him forty times what would happen if Chad came home. They didn't get it. Of course Chad was going to show up sometime—he always did after one of his playboy disappearing acts. Mac knew that perfectly well when he'd asked her to marry him, known she'd loved his brother, too. Those sticky complications didn't erase the reasons for the marriage, but the opposite. Kelly had been in danger. Cut-and-dried. And Mac loved his brother, but he knew him. Painfully well. Whether Chad was snoozing on a beach in Jamaica or right here made no difference. Mac couldn't trust his brother to protect Kelly or to do right by the child. Keeping her safe was up to him.

And that was precisely why his response to that damn hug was so inexcusable. Mac shoveled a hand through his hair. He remembered folding his arms around her, because he couldn't just stand there like a lump, and hell, he didn't want her feeling rejected or scared. Returning the hug seemed an okay thing to do, but after that it all got hazy. Sensations had bombarded him like bullets. Soft bullets...like her hair tickling his nose, and the feel of her tummy pressing against him, and the way her skin glowed so vulnerably in the firelight. She smelled like peach shampoo and soap and that teasing, illusive perfume she wore. It bugged him, those self-deprecating comments she made about being graceless and as big as an elephant. She wasn't. She'd felt so small in his arms, so warm, so real. He remembered closing his eyes, remembered feeling gut-punched with a stupid, alien, childish wave of longing...he also remembered, too well, being aroused faster than a trigger-hot teenage boy.

He'd jerked back faster than a whiplash, hoping she hadn't noticed. But all night long he'd seen the bathroom light go on and off. He'd worried about her pregnant kidneys, worried she was sick. But mostly he'd worried that she couldn't sleep because she was in a strange house with her whole life turned upside down, and now he'd become a new kind of unknown worry in that picture for her, too.

He was just going to have to fix it, that was all. Hell,

he'd handled multimillion dollar mergers, European stock crashes, hiring and firing staff in four countries. How much trouble could one pip-squeak-size pregnant woman be?

And then suddenly she was in the doorway. "Morning, Mac. You're up so early. Whew, can you believe all this snow?"

"Good morning back and yeah, some of those drifts outside are really something." Oh, God, one look and he could feel a sinking. Give him a stock crash anytime. He *knew* what to do about that kind of thing.

No matter how glaringly lit the kitchen was, she was still a brighter shock of color. She smiled at him through a sleepy yawn. Her hair was brushed—he was pretty sure—but it still fell around her shoulders in tumbled swirls. An oversize red sweatshirt burgeoned over her tummy, the color matching the two dots of color on her cheeks and her pants both. Unless he was mistaken, she was wearing fat fluffy hound dogs on her feet. It occurred to him that they must be slippers. And that five-hundred-watt sleepy smile suddenly disappeared—hell, had he already done something wrong?

She motioned around the kitchen. "Oh, Mac. You've gone to so much trouble—"

"No trouble at all," he said swiftly. "I just figured you might be hungry for breakfast—"

"I'm always hungry, but I'm afraid I get a queasy stomach first thing in the morning. The most I can handle is a little juice and toast—"

"Toast." The one thing, naturally, that he hadn't thought of. "No problem, I know we've got bread around here somewhere—"

She shuffled in, motioning him to relax. "Now don't be silly. You don't have to wait on me, and I have to start finding my way around the kitchen besides. And listen, I'll help you do something with all that food—"

"No, no, just sit down and relax." Best to steer her away from the stove and all that food, particularly if there was a threat of her throwing up. "Did you sleep okay?"

"Pretty good—except for the baby kicking. And I had a little problem with the mattress…"

"The mattress?" His head jerked up from where he was pouring her juice.

"Uh-huh. I don't think I'm cut out for a life of affluence. I could hardly sleep on a mattress with no lumps."

He'd made a whole list of stuff he thought she'd need. Somehow he'd never considered that she'd want a mattress with lumps.

"Um, Mac…maybe you want to stop pouring that cranberry juice on the table?"

"Oh. Oh, my God…"

But she was laughing as she unfurled a long skirt of paper towels and carried them to the table to start mopping. "That was a joke about the lumpy mattress. I was trying to be funny. But I'm afraid I'm making you nervous—"

"I'm not nervous," he assured her, thinking how little she knew him. The whole family could testify that he had nerves of steel. The tougher the crisis, the calmer he got. Problems were his baliwick. Yet somehow when his new wife discovered some spilled cranberry juice on him and started patting his chest, Mac could feel nervous heat shoot up his neck.

Kelly stepped back and glanced at his face. "Listen, you. We're going to talk about this, and we're going to make both of us more comfortable, I swear."

Mac thought: that was supposed to be his line. And he was the one who had planned on using that firm, calm, take-charge tone of voice. Hound-dog slippers or no hound-dog slippers, the woman was downright bossy. Efficiently she finished mopping, retrieved the bread from a cabinet and then gravely pulled out a pad of paper and a ballpoint pen from her pocket.

"You're a list-maker?"

"Can't start the day without one," she admitted.

Maybe there was hope for this morning yet...and since she was showing off hers, Mac figured he might as well show off his. His list, however, covered the serious things. The security system. Emergency numbers. How to run the electronics in the house from computers to VCRs. Credit cards and her new checkbook.

Only Kelly was suddenly frowning. "Mac, I realize we have to cover all that life stuff, but could we just talk about important things for a minute?" She already had her ballpoint poised, ready to scribble. "What are your favorite foods?"

"Foods?" The irrelevant question seemed to come from nowhere.

"Yeah. You like steaks or fish? Anything you're allergic to, or vegetables you can't stand? Are you watching your cholesterol or just praying you're immortal? Any special desserts you like?"

"Kelly, I don't expect you to cook—"

"What, we're going to eat by osmosis? And then there's your favorite TV shows. And more important than that— when's your goof-off time?"

"Goof-off time?"

"Your job's a steam cooker. You don't need to tell me that. But what do you do to relax? Loll in a Jacuzzi? Hike? Mellow out in front of the tube? Ski? And is there a time of day you need some space alone to unwind?" She hesitated. "What's wrong? Why are you looking at me that way?"

Mac didn't realize he'd been looking at her in any specific way. Her nonstop bubbling questions were just hard to keep up with. And so, he kept discovering, was she. "I just can't remember anyone ever asking me about my goof-off time. And I don't think my own sister knows what my favorite foods are.''

"Well, Chloe isn't living with you. I am. And I don't want to intrude where you don't want me, Mac, but obviously this is going to go easier if we know something about each other's living habits. You like your shirts starched?''

"Damned if I know. They go to a cleaners. They come back. I always sort of thought it was a magic thing. Nobody ever told me there were choices.''

She muttered some humorous comment about *men!* and then rattled on. And on. Mac kept waiting for her to ask about money—hell, no one ever had a conversation with him without asking about money, and Kelly actually needed to know about household accounts and where the cash was. She asked him what he liked to read. He needed her to know how to page him wherever he was. She had a "need to know" section on her list, too, consisting of irrelevant issues such as whether he was bugged by unwanted phone calls she could field for him.

Mac couldn't remember such a bewildering conversation. Nobody ever asked him personal questions. He hadn't even thought about such things in years. And of course he catered to her. If it killed him, he was going to cater to her. She was not only pregnant, but she'd had nonstop traumas in her life in the last few weeks, and he was damn well going to make her life both easy and safe—even if he had to do it over her dead body.

"Now don't get exasperated, Mac. I'm almost through...."

"I'm *not* exasperated. I *never* get exasperated.''

"Uh-huh. Actually that was on my list...what kinds of things test your patience? But actually, I think I'm going to have no trouble figuring that out on my own.'' That impish grin of hers could inspire a hard-core grouch, but again it was gone faster than smoke. "I *have* to bring up one unpleasant thing, though, so brace yourself. It's money."

Finally. He knew she had to have a practical bone somewhere in that curly blond head.

"Cards on the table, Mac."

"Cards on the table," he agreed.

She took a breath. "I haven't balanced a checkbook in twenty-seven years. I finally accepted that it isn't going to happen. I got A's in English and history, but you put a bunch of figures in front of me and I'm dead. I just thought I'd better be honest with you. Don't waste your time trying to talk figures or money with me. It just goes in one ear and out the other."

"Kelly, that's okay. You don't have to balance any checkbooks. But there really are a few things we should talk about related to this—"

A flush suddenly streaked up her cheeks. "Excuse me for just a minute, would you?"

He could have guessed a call of nature would interrupt the first moment they touched on anything serious. He rested his head in his hands until she came back from the bathroom, thinking he'd better preserve his strength. Nothing was going as he planned. Nothing. If she had some resistance to talking about finances, that could wait, but so far she'd wasted this whole conversation talking about an irrelevant subject—namely him. They had to get off boring topics and get to some meat. The instant she emerged from the bathroom, he hustled to get the first word in. "Could I have a turn at *my* list now?"

"Well, sure, Mac."

She *said* "sure," but unlike the way he'd patiently, politely sat still for all her confounding questions, she started flying around the kitchen. Pots and pans clattered. Water ran. Silverware dropped.

"Kelly, I'll do that cleanup later. These are serious health questions—"

"But didn't I already tell you this? My ob-gyn doctor is Dr. Lynn. She's a peach. And my health insurance is through the Fortune company—which I'd think you'd already know is terrific." Again, she lubbered his brain with one of those female-devil sassy grins. But again, that smile of hers died faster than smoke. "Holy cow, I never thought to ask—I don't lose my health insurance because of being married to you, do I? That doesn't disappear because we're suddenly related now?"

"The employee insurance you had still works after you quit, because the pregnancy was a preexisting condition. And you're now covered under mine. And neither question is relevant. Kel, could you try and get it in your head that we're not destitute? You don't have to worry about things like that anymore."

"Well, I realize you have money, but I've always paid my own bills. It doesn't seem right to take advantage of you, Mac."

God. Most women seemed to grasp swiftly that an association with him was worth gravy. Kelly was not only independent; he doubted she could spell "greed" with a big print dictionary. "You're not taking advantage of me—and could we stick to the subject of health? You had an ultrasound not long ago?"

"The beginning of last week," she affirmed. "Initially they weren't sure about twins. Because they run in your family, the chance was obviously higher—"

He knew. And that was how his mother had died, giving birth to the twins, a fear he'd never wanted to voice to Kelly for fear of scaring her.

"—But there's just one baby. And the little one's doing terrific. Perfect. Growing just as it should. The due date's the end of February, and I didn't ask the sex. It really doesn't matter to me if it's a boy or a girl, but I'm having a tough time picking out names. I'm thinking of Anne for a girl. Oops. You don't like that name?''

"I like it fine."

"From your expression—"

"Annie was my mother's name." He took a breath. "And something tells me you already knew that."

She nodded. "Kate mentioned it to me one time. And Marie another time. Both your aunts thought a lot of your mom, Mac. She sounded like she was a really special and wonderful woman. And I loved the name, so I just thought I'd try it out on you...sometimes people don't like to use names already in the family, but—"

"You couldn't possibly have come up with a name that meant more to mc."

Her smile was joyful. "So that's terrific. One name settled. We just have to argue about a boy's name then—"

"Which we can do. Later. But somehow every time I ask you about health, you sidetrack to the baby and you never answer a single question—"

"Oh, me. There's just nothing interesting to say. I'm fine. Except that Doc Lynn said I had skinny hips. Can you believe that, when I'm fat as a slug?"

"You're not a slug, you're not an elephant—I don't know why you keep saying stuff like that when you're not remotely fat. You're beautiful. But what does that 'skinny hips' mean? Is there a health risk for you with the delivery?"

"Mac, I'm not the least bit beautiful. You don't have to do those ego stroke kind of things with me."

By then he was feeding pans into the dishwasher, because he could hardly let her do all the k.p. while he sat like a lazy worm with his list. But she was standing right next to him, whipping plastic wrap around some bowls, and he couldn't believe she was that blind about herself. No, of course she wasn't beautiful the way models were classically beautiful. But models were cold. Those blue eyes of hers were so huge and emotive they could stop a guy in his tracks. Her mouth reminded him of strawberries; her skin was as pure as a translucent pearl…it wasn't as if any one thing made her beautiful, but her expressions were so full of life and sensuality and emotion. Surely she had to realize how attractive she was. A man can hardly help imagining how that soft skin would feel all bare against his on a nice, big, hard mattre…abruptly Mac pulled himself up short. What the hell was the matter with him? Thinking about his wife that way?

Impatiently he shoved a frying pan into the dishwasher. "Could we get back to the question—did the obstetrician tell you there were any special health risks for you with the delivery?"

"Nope. I'm fit as a fiddle. Although talking about this reminds me…" She glanced out the window. "It's pretty obvious we're snowed in, but do you think we'll be cleared out by tomorrow night?"

"What's tomorrow night?"

"My Lamaze class. Six-thirty. It won't kill me to miss it, but there are four in all, and so far I've only been to the first one—"

"We'll get you there. Don't worry about it." He hesitated. "Were you planning on going alone?"

"Yes. Mollie offered to be my labor coach. So did Amanda—you know her, she works for your cousin in marketing? Actually Kate offered to be my coach, too…your aunt has been so wonderful to me, and like Kate put it, she went through labor a half dozen times herself, so who could possibly be more help? But…well, I didn't want to hurt anyone's feelings, but I'd just rather do this alone."

Mac sensed this was touchy ground. "As often as I've heard women in the family talk about this stuff, I admit I wasn't listening very hard. This 'coach' is like a person who supports you when you're going through labor?''

"Yeah, that's the idea."

"And you don't want anyone with you?"

"Having some support sounds good in theory, but the truth is, I'm lousy with pain. A real sissy," she said cheerfully. "The woman who leads the class does this big cheerleading talk about the joy of giving birth. I'm not buying that Brooklyn Bridge. The baby's going to be a joy, but I figure the labor is never going to make my top ten list of fun things. And I just figured out a long time ago, I handle tough things best when I'm alone."

Mac didn't like the idea of her going through serious pain alone. He liked the idea of her learning to handle the tough things alone in life even less. But he also didn't figure his name would even cross Kelly's mind as a support person. Hell, he was just her husband.

Out of nowhere, she suddenly reached out and put her hand on his stomach. So much for husbandlike thoughts. His pulse bucked to a sudden pagan, drumroll beat that snapped every hormone he owned to attention. His gaze shot from her splayed fingers on his abdomen to her face. Then he realized she was just pushing him out of the way— the way a wife would do. She had a box of dishwasher soap in the other hand and just wanted to pour it in and turn on the machine.

He got out of the way. "That coach thing is up to you, but if it's all right, I'd like to go to the Lamaze class."

"You want to learn how to grunt and groan?" she asked humorously.

"I'd like to get a clue what you're going to go through, and I know zip about babies or labor now. Would you mind if I went with you?"

"No, no problem. As long as you really want to, and

aren't feeling obligated…listen, how do you feel about oat-meal-raisin cookies?''

"Pardon?"

"We're snowed in. Seems a great day to make cookies to me. And I decided on a bedroom upstairs for the nurs-ery—the far one, next to the peach bathroom?''

"Fine. Whatever you want." He poured himself another cup of coffee, thinking labor, cookies, nurseries…now that Ms. Efficiency had leveled the kitchen, she was back to talking about a zillion subjects at once. He sipped the hot brew, figuring he was going to need the caffeine.

"Is it okay if I put a fresh coat of paint on the walls?"

The caffeine helped. He was prepared for another new subject to pop out of nowhere. "No."

"No? I realize that there's nothing wrong with the paint, Mac, but it's really a dark blue. I just thought for a baby's room it needs to be some kind of light, happy color—''

"I wasn't objecting to the room being painted. You want any rooms painted or changed, we'll get it done. But you don't need to be lifting heavy paint cans on your own."

She argued. She liked painting. She wanted to do it her-self. Pregnancy wasn't an illness and she didn't need cod-dling. Yadda yadda, on and on. At some point in the dis-cussion she plopped a bowl in his lap and ordered him to stir. Apparently it was the oatmeal-raisin batter—and it stirred about as easily as cement—yet from nowhere Mac suddenly realized this strange thing. He hadn't thought of work or responsibilities in hours. He was sitting in a tipped-back chair with a foot propped on a rung. He was not only stirring cookie batter, but he could actually feel a grin molding the corners of his mouth.

Relaxed hadn't been a word in his vocabulary in years. He liked stress and power and responsibilities. But it never occurred to him that anything about this marriage could be easy. He had no idea what living with Kelly would be like—except for respecting that she'd been trapped into making the best choice she had, no different from him. But he'd never expected...her. A woman who chattered nonstop and had an irrepressible giggle and made the whole house rock with motion and light. She teased him. She ordered him around. She didn't have a formal bone in her entire body.

For a moment, he just wished it would keep snowing, that the whole world would disappear for a little longer.

For a moment, it almost seemed as if he was a real husband, and she belonged to him, and there was nothing more natural on earth than being with her.

But then, of course, the phone rang.

The real world intruded and the foolish illusion vanished. Mac had a job in this relationship. To keep her safe. She'd never chosen to be with him—and he warned himself that it would be dangerous to pretend otherwise.

Four

Thirty hours later, Kelly was pulling a cherry red maternity top over her head and considering divorce. The honeymoon had only lasted through one batch of cookies. Once the phone started ringing yesterday morning…well, she wasn't able to eavesdrop well enough to pick up any details about the problem, but it was something about a guy named Gray McGuire and a threat of some takeover. Mac had been on the company jet, flying to New York, less than an hour after that.

She sat on the bed and pulled on fresh socks—an increasingly challenging task with the size of her tummy—and she needed to hustle. Five minutes from now she needed to be in the car, en route to her Lamaze class if she were going to make it on time. Going alone didn't bother her. Mac was a busy man. She'd never believed he wanted to go to the class with her anyway.

The crisis with her marriage had nothing to do with her

new groom being absent. It wasn't even remotely Mac's fault, but that didn't make the problem any less serious.

Kelly conquered the socks and then looked wildly around for a hairbrush. She'd just moved her stuff into the corner blue-and-white bedroom this morning, and she kept forgetting where she'd put things. Like hairbrushes. And shoes. She'd just located one shoe—and the brush—when she suddenly heard the sound of a truck engine below. Curiously she peeked out the window and saw a moving van.

Still hopping into her shoes, she hurried down the hall to the stairs. "Martha? Did you see that truck outsi—?"

Mac's housekeeper was already charging for the front door, her steel gray bun bobbing at the pace of her jog. "I saw. Don't you worry about a thing, dear. Mr. Fortune just arranged for more of your things to get moved from your old apartment. I realize you have to leave for your class, and I'll make sure everything gets inside safely—"

"What things?" Kelly asked in bewilderment, but once Martha opened the front door, she had a clear view of the truck bed outside. Against the snowy landscape her pink couch was a noticeable shock of color. "Holy kamoly. Martha, I never asked Mac to move any of the furniture. There's no possible way any of those things are going to fit in here—"

"Now, don't stand in the draft, dear. You don't want to catch cold with the baby. And Mr. Fortune said not to let you lift anything, so it's just as well you need to be leaving right now...there you are, Benz. He's got the car all warmed up—"

Kelly whirled around. "Benz, you're not driving me."

"Sure I am, miss. You don't want to be battling that snow. And Mr. Fortune says I'm to drive you wherever you want to go, and see you get in as well. Now we've got plenty of time, but we do need to leave—you just let Martha worry about the moving van, all righty?"

No, it wasn't all righty. The whole drive into town, Kelly huffed in the seat next to Benz. Maybe the words "Mr. Fortune said" would hit most people as innocuous—and certainly nothing to cause a crisis in a marriage. But for the last thirty hours, Kelly must have heard the phrase at least fifty-million times. Martha and Benz were the retired married couple who lived at the edge of Mac's property. They only worked part-time, but the close living relationship enabled Mac to have certain things done—like repairs or plumbing or heavy cleaning—because the couple could pop in to supervise while he was working.

They were both darlings. But from the instant Mac had left for New York, Kelly had been subjected to a steady stream of Mr. Fortune said this and Mr. Fortune said that. "Mr. Fortune said I should ask whatever you want to eat and that you're not to worry about cooking." "Mr. Fortune said you're not to lift any boxes." A painter had telephoned. "Mr. Fortune said you needed some rooms done." Mollie had called yesterday but Kelly had accidentally fallen asleep on the couch. Martha later told her that "Mr. Fortune said" she wasn't to be interrupted any time she might be resting.

"There are going to be changes—*bbbiiigggg* changes— if this marriage is going to survive," Kelly muttered.

"What'd you say, miss?"

"I said it's absolutely ridiculous for you to get dragged out in the cold with your arthritis when I could have driven myself perfectly well alone."

"Well, now, it's not a question of your being capable of driving, honey, it's just that Mr. Fortune said—"

"I know, I know." Princesses in ivory towers couldn't be more coddled than this, she thought darkly. She'd never expected so much attention from Mac—much less that he could pull off this protectiveness long distance. And to a point, she didn't mind. Being pampered wasn't her cup of tea, but after the attack, she just couldn't seem to feel safe. Between the security system and Mac's support staff, those fears were fading like smoke. That wasn't the aspect of the "Mr. Fortune saids" that really troubled her.

It was Mac she was worried about. For Pete's sake, everybody treated him like a god. Of the zillion people who called the house, there wasn't one who didn't ask for Mr. Fortune instead of Mac. What kind of life was he living, with all these people kowtowing all the time? Benz and Martha clearly felt affection for him. It wasn't that. His family obviously cared, too. But nobody called to say "hi." They all called because they wanted something from him. And Kelly didn't know whether he chose that formal distance or it had been forced on him, but it bothered her, badly, that absolutely no one seemed close to Mac.

"And it's not like I expected him to sit around and eat cookies. But for heaven's sake, he can't even count on a holiday to put his feet up and relax."

"You talking to yourself again, Kelly?"

"Now don't start thinking I need a straitjacket, Benz. A little insanity's allowed in pregnant women. But I'm telling you we need to make some changes in his life, and I'm serious about that."

Benz seemed motivated to agree with anything she said, no matter how goofy, but that changed when they pulled up in front of the clinic. "I'm watching until you get in. And you wait inside the door, now, when the class is over. Don't be going outside. I'll come in and get you—"

"Sheesh, I will. Quit with the orders." She bussed Benz on the cheek—if he was going to behave like an honorary grandfather, then he was going to get treated like one—and then heaved her bulky girth out of the car.

The stinging cold slapped her face, but it was only a short walk into the clinic. The snow was shoveled so high from the holiday blizzard that mini white mountains framed the sidewalks. Other women were hustling toward the door at the same time, and she recognized most of the faces from the first class. A spirit of camaraderie had caught on swiftly, because they had so many things in common. They were all first-time moms, all bigger than boats, all waddling at the speed and all dressed in the same kind of easy comfortable clothes to accommodate sitting on floor mats for the exercises.

Everyone else, though, had brought a coach—mostly husbands, but a couple of the women had brought friends or sisters. Kelly felt a pang of isolation, even knowing that being alone was her own choice, but she just couldn't imagine asking anyone—especially Mac—to help her through this. She'd made her own bed when she'd fallen for a man like Chad. Her baby wasn't a mistake, but what she'd done certainly was, and she just hadn't felt right about asking anyone else to pay her prices with her.

Those disquieting thoughts faded away as she joined the other women pouring into the classroom. Everyone was laughing and chattering as coats got heaped on the floor and the group settled down on floor mats. Mrs. Riley was already standing at the head of the class, looking more like a zesty thirty-year-old than the fifty she had to be. The nurse was so full of enthusiasm that personally Kelly thought she could sell the Brooklyn Bridge several times over. No labor war stories were allowed. Mrs. Riley was hot for all of them to believe that giving birth was going to be more fun than a party.

"All right, ladies. You can see I brought a tableful of dolls tonight. We're going to practice diapering and burping skills and all the things you need to know about taking care of a newborn. After that, we'll practice our breathing exercises...."

Once Mrs. Riley verbally wound up on lecture mode, she always had a tough time winding down. Yet Kelly heard the teacher's voice suddenly falter before going on. One head turned toward the doorway, then another. By the time Kelly realized a new face had entered the classroom, a pair of wing tip shoes had already made their way to her side. Mac. He hunkered down next to her in a navy suit and starched white shirt, looking as if he were an exotic panther in a room full of plump wrens. His attire was totally unlike everyone else's casual clothes, but that wasn't why every female eye in the place zoned on him.

Something curled in her stomach. She couldn't name the emotion disturbing her pulse, but it had nothing to do with recognizing he was a hunk, nothing to do with startled surprise that he could possibly be here. Maybe it was just realizing that he'd been "Mr. Fortune" all these months for her no different than for everyone else...but not anymore. He'd become Mac, a man she knew well enough to notice the tired circles under his eyes, to worry whether he'd caught enough food or sleep. And she was aware that his air of command had aroused the other women's interest—no mean feat, considering that some of the women were close to term and had verbally sworn off sex and men for the rest of their lives. But Mac seemed oblivious to creating that little stir when he walked in, which struck Kelly as more telling evidence that her husband was alone. Really alone, no matter where he was. And used to it.

"I'm sorry I'm late," he murmured next to her ear.

"I never expected you to make it at all—"

"I told you I would."

Apparently Mac thought that settled it. He'd given her his word. "But I thought you were in New York. And that takeover thing sounded a huge problem—"

"It is. But it'll still be there tomorrow." He shagged the knot on his tie to loosen it, and whispered, "Can you fill me in on what we're doing here so I'm not in disgrace on the first test?"

She hadn't forgotten the class. It was just temporarily she couldn't seem to pay attention to anyone else in the universe. "You sicced a painter on me."

"Uh-huh. Nice guy, got four kids of his own. I can guarantee he won't let you lift a thing. And I know you told me you wanted to paint the room yourself. My theory on that problem was to see how you took to bribery. You can win the next ten arguments if you let me win that one."

"You think I'm buying that Las Vegas dollar?" His gaze was roaming her face, making her nervous. There was nothing sexual between them—she'd already told herself that several dozen times. And she knew he felt responsible for her, so he was just probably studying her to make sure she didn't look sick or overtired or something.

"How's our baby today?"

"Our baby's doing wonderful, but I'd better warn you before you get home, I don't get the security system, Mac. I set it off twice today. Really goofed it up. I'm sorry, Benz and Martha went over and over it with me, but—"

"Don't worry about it. I'll go over it with you. And you'll get it, Kel."

The crazy thought occurred to her that she could probably get anything if Mac kept looking at her that way. Like he cared. Like she meant something to him. Like he wasn't quite sure what the sam hill this woman was doing in his life, but he wanted to be right here, next to her, figuring it out.

Kelly told herself to get a grip; she knew perfectly well the pregnancy had a kaflooey effect on her hormones...but then Mrs. Riley's strident voice helpfully smacked her back to reality.

"Miss Sinclair? I really don't want you to miss any of the material we're covering tonight—"

Mac quietly responded before Kelly could. "It's Mrs. Fortune now, not Miss Sinclair."

"Mrs. Fortune," the teacher echoed. The way her posture perked up, it was pretty clear she recognized the last name. "And you are—?"

"Her husband. And we apologize for talking and interrupting the class. I'm hoping you won't give us a detention if we don't do it again."

That brought a laugh, but the rest of the class was an unsettling experience. Mrs. Riley had a basket of dolls set up at the front of the room. She illustrated a variety of things, from diapering to burping techniques to the safe methods of holding a newborn, and then let the class loose with the life-size dolls to practice. Mac waded in with everyone else.

His first diapering attempt looked brilliant, except when he lifted the doll, the diaper fell off. His look of total bewilderment made her chuckle, but when he tried again, his brow furrowed in intense concentration as if mastering this diapering business were on a par with finding a solution to world peace. Four tries later, he shot her a triumphant grin—the diaper had stayed on. Only he abruptly seemed to realize that everyone else had finished and were back down on the mats except for him and Kelly.

"Oops," he murmured. "You seem to be stuck with the dunce of the class. How's your patience level with slow learners?"

"Are you kidding? We'll have the best diapered baby on the block. But it does seem like you might have just a teensy perfectionist streak..."

"Me?"

Cripes, he made her chuckle again, and she thought *Darn you, Kelly, don't you dare fall in love with him.* It wasn't as if he never told her about his willingness to be a dad, but she just assumed he was coming from a sense of responsibility. Not that he meant it from the heart. Yet he listened to Mrs. Riley as if her words were worth gold. He took notes. He burped the doll with such a dead serious expression that two beads of sweat broke out on his brow. He studiously absorbed the information about "cradle cap" as if nothing could possibly interest him more.

Darn it, he was darling. And his treating her with such sensitivity and perception had already ransomed a corner of her heart, but this was worse. Possibly the baby was going to be grown up and driving before Mac figured out diapers—he was just a *tad* on the perfectionist side—but the thought kept pouncing in her mind that he was going to be a preciously loving dad.

Mrs. Riley put the class through their breathing exercises, then let them go—after announcing that the last class would show a movie of a live birth; coaches needed to be sure to come as well as the expecting moms.

"You don't have to go to that last class if seeing something like that would make you uncomfortable," Kelly told him as they put on coats and headed outside.

"Now I know you said you didn't want a coach, but unless you object, I'd still like to attend whatever classes are left. I wasn't kidding about knowing nothing about babies, Kel. I'm an uncle several times over, but you know my family. The women all cluster around the kids. The guys don't have a chance." He pushed the door open, and hooked an arm around her shoulder when he saw the slippery walk outside.

The icy night wind burned her cheeks, but she felt protected and snuggled against Mac's shoulder. "I see your car instead of Benz's, so I assume you managed to connect with him—"

"Yeah, I reached him on the car phone, so he'd know I was picking you up."

"Did you have a chance to eat dinner?"

"I'll just catch something when we get home."

She hesitated. Between the flying back and forth and all

the heavy business—and his hustling to keep his word about making the class—she suspected he could have missed lunch as well as dinner. "There's a really good place just a block from here, if you don't mind plain cooking—"

"It's okay, Kel. I know you have to be tired."

She was tired, but it was just "pregnancy tired." She woke up ready to snooze; it wasn't as if she'd overdone anything that day. And so far she hadn't caught Mac confessing to one need for himself, which left her no recourse except sneakery. "Mac?"

"What?"

She tried out her most innocent expression. "I'm awfully hungry myself."

Mac immediately walked faster. "Well, heck, you should have said."

Less than twenty minutes later, he had a giant plate of lasagna in front of him and was diving in like a starving wolf. This late, they almost had the quiet ma-and-pa restaurant to themselves. If the place had a decor, it was early-family. The specialty was home cooking; the cook was singing in the back, and photos of the real ma and pa's grandchildren were displayed behind the register. So were the freshly baked desserts, which Kelly had noticed before Mac.

"Don't tell me you're not going to have a nightmare from that." He motioned to the plates in front of her—a giant piece of lemon meringue pie with a side order of pickles.

"The baby loves pickles," she assured him. "Preferably kosher dills, but at two in the morning, the baby isn't usually too picky."

"And does the baby usually prefer that you eat your pickles with lemon meringue pie?"

"Well, I'd rather have the pickles with a toasted almond

ice-cream bar, but they're hard to find. Lemon meringue pie will do in a pinch. I don't know how you can resist a slice—''

''Maybe later. Right now I'm having too much fun watching you indulge,'' Mac said dryly. ''Is this an example of an expectant mom's food cravings?''

Mostly she was enjoying watching him inhale the homemade lasagna—there was no question he'd been starving. ''I always thought the food cravings were an old wives' tale, and I can't believe I fell for pickles. It's such a cliché. Would you believe I always hated pickles before I got pregnant?''

''You could have fooled me.''

''Now I take nutrition for the baby seriously. But my mom had this theory…if a pregnant woman craved some food, maybe there's something in that food that the baby really needs.''

''I think that's a fascinating justification for being a pickle addict.''

She grinned. ''It could be worse. One of the women in the class is hot for snails.''

''Oh, God. How about if we don't put that idea in your head, okay?''

They didn't linger after eating, but by the time they walked back to his car, she had him laughing. The sound hit her ears like riches. She'd never really heard him laugh before…Mac just never seemed to forget his responsibilities long enough to unbend and have some fun. A rare feeling of feminine power made her feel buoyant. She'd done something good for him, and it showed in his looselimbed stride and the smile crinkles around his eyes.

On the ride home, he turned more serious, but the stiffness between them was gone. It was as if that laughter had broken some emotional ice, and talking seriously was more like confiding. ''For an hour-long class, I kind of caught an earful. Some of the women were talking about developing high blood pressure and prenatal diabetes and—"

She hustled to cut those worries off at the pass. "I don't have any of those high risks, Mac. The only health problem that's developed for me with this pregnancy is greed. I've got an appetite that won't quit. And a lot of those health problems tend to run in families. My mom had an easy birth. So should I."

"Well, not to ask a personal question, but did your mom happen to have those infamous 'skinny hips'?"

"Maybe not skinny, but she was on the slender side. I realize this must take a great leap of faith to believe, but I swear I'm normally smaller than the Titanic myself."

"Give it up, Tiny. Your only credit to fame is that tummy. So...where'd you grow up?"

The heat started kicking in. The flashing city lights faded once Mac turned off onto the darker, quieter country roads. Feeling cocooned in a private world with him made her feel more comfortable talking. She named the neighborhood where she'd grown up, which was about a planet difference from where he had. "I've never made a secret of being illegitimate, Mac. I never knew my dad—he took off on my mom about thirty seconds after she told him she was pregnant. His loss. My mom really had to struggle financially to make it, but every memory I have of her is precious. I never doubted for a second that I was loved. She was an incredible person."

"You miss her."

Kelly nodded. "Yes, but the way I miss her has changed. When she first died, I thought I'd die, too...but somehow over time the same memories that first hurt the most are the ones I love to remember now. You lost your mom, too—"

"Yes. And I know exactly what you mean. The grief was overwhelming when she first died. But now when those memories come back, it's like she's part of me, right there. I'm just sorry Chad and Chloe never had the years with her that I did.''

She hesitated. There were things she'd tried to tell Mac about Chad before, but his brother was inevitably an uncomfortable, touchy subject between them. Possibly there was no way it could be otherwise, but while they were talking so easily, it seemed a good time to get some things out in the air that needed clearing up.

''When I was growing up, it was a big thing with me...not wanting to disappoint my mother. She did so much and she never complained. But she was also really strict...like makeup was forbidden. I always had a ten o'clock curfew, and I worked from the time I was a teenager so there'd be few chances to date. She wasn't mean about the rules, it was just that she felt so strongly—the one thing in life she didn't want me to do was get pregnant before I was married the way she did.''

Mac glanced at her. ''Kelly, that's a mistake people have been making since the beginning of time. It happens. Everyone's human.''

''I realize that, but...'' She hesitated again. ''Mac, when you asked me to marry you, I told you at the time it was over between me and Chad. Once he took off on me, I would never have married him. But I'm not sure if you really believed me—''

''I believe my brother hurt you. But however you feel or felt about him, the night you were assaulted in the parking lot changed all the circumstances.''

''Yes. Completely. But...I've still felt badly about this whole situation making things awkward for you and your brother. It took two to make that mistake. I don't want you thinking that it was all Chad's fault. He couldn't have known how green I was. Any other woman my age would have known something about men, not been so naïve. He gave me a rush—that's no crime. I misinterpreted his feelings—that wasn't his fault, either. He said more than once that he wasn't interested in children, and by the time he took off—Mac, I couldn't have married him by then anyway. There was no way it could have worked. But I don't believe he ever meant to hurt me. Or use me. We were just playing by entirely different rules."

Mac didn't immediately respond, and by then they were pulling into the driveway. This far away from the city, the night was breathless, the sky studded with diamond stars and the silver half-moon veiled with a cotton puff cloud. When he parked by the front door, he climbed out first, and then hiked around to open her side. She'd have opened her own door, except that these days it always took some time to free herself from the seat belt and get her tummy organized enough to maneuver.

When he hadn't immediately pursued the conversation about Chad, she assumed coming home had either distracted him or he didn't want to talk about it. But as he reached in a hand to help her out, he said quietly, "Kelly, he's coming home sometime. You know that."

"Yes."

"I don't know what you're going to feel when you see him again. But you said you were worried about my relationship with Chad, and I'm well aware the whole family seems determined to see this as an awkward situation. Don't be worried. There's nothing awkward for me. For me, the facts are clear. He slept with you and took off. He hurt you. I love him—he's my brother—I also know that he has problems that I just don't understand, but he was still raised with a sense of honor, and what he did to you was dead wrong."

Kelly swallowed. "I don't want you angry with him because of me—"

''Then you lose, Tiny. Because I intend to mop the floor with him.''

''Mac, you're not listening to a thing I said. It took two to get me in trouble. And maybe it took his disappearing for me to realize what a mistake I made, but that's water over the dam. It's over. I was dumb. But my being so incredibly dumb wasn't your brother's fault.''

''Would you quit worrying? I'm not going to kill him. I'm just going to annihilate him. It's an entirely different thing.''

Mac suddenly seemed to hear the way his words came out, because his grave expression abruptly turned comically confused. She couldn't explain why she impulsively hooked her arms around his neck. At that instant, she simply had to. Because of that bead of sweat on his forehead when he'd been trying to master diapering a doll. Because of bullying her long distance with all the insufferable coddling. Because of all those ''Mr. Fortune saids'' that made her worry that nobody loved him. Because of calling her Tiny. Because he really was an old-fashioned heroic man who believed in honor and lived what he believed in.

Because she thought Mac needed a kiss.

The impulse made perfect sense to her. But her husband responded as if a tiger had just been spotted prowling the property. He went as still as stone when her arms climbed around his shoulders, carefully didn't move when she surged up on tiptoe. Mac, being Mac, was too much a gentleman to reject her. Or maybe he thought the danger would go away if he was careful not to move.

Kelly hadn't known there was any danger. She certainly hadn't realized there were tigers prowling their personal property. Obviously she was aware that Mac scrabbled her hormones, but that was hardly a newsworthy item—Mac could scrabble the hormones of a ninety-year-old nun. She was afraid he'd respond with humiliating kindness if he realized she was attracted to him. As far as she knew, that was a well-kept secret, and there was absolutely nothing on her mind but affection at that moment.

Only that moment passed. And everything changed. His lips were initially as cold as the snowflakes that stung her cheeks, but his lips warmed up so fast. He tasted dark and exotic. He tasted alluring. He tasted like something she'd longed for and never found before him.

Even through the barrier of her down jacket, she felt his hands suddenly clench her waist, maybe because he intended to push her away. But he didn't. His hands skimmed, then slowly shivered around to her back until he was holding her no different than she was holding him. His mouth brushed hers like a soft stroke of satin, but that changed, too. The pressure of the kiss deepened, darkened, as if heat and smoke had been trapped inside Mac for a long time and the fire was suddenly let loose.

She'd known he was alone, seen it, sensed it, but she wasn't sure Mac had a clue how wildly, painfully lonely he'd been. She closed her eyes and kissed him back, her pulse rushing, rushing, emotions clambering in her heart—the need to give, to hold, to protect this man who wasn't supposed to need any of those things. For sure, she'd never imagined he could need her. Yet his vulnerability swept her under, made an ice-cold night transform into a magically wondrous place. His head surged up for air, yet he dipped right back down another kiss, this one involving tongues and teeth, this one waking up a whole brood of tigers....

Her jacket was gaping open, because as of two weeks ago she couldn't zip it anymore. Still, there were bunches of winter clothes between them. So many that he couldn't touch her in any intimate way, yet her breasts tightened and swelled with a sweet-hot ache and desire-coiled heat deep in the center of her. Her tummy tucked against him and her fingers knuckled tight at her nape, willing him not to stop kissing her, willing this moment to never end. Her being with him made sense, heart-sense, like nothing had been right in her life before this and everything suddenly was.

The baby suddenly kicked. Hard. Hard enough that she surfaced from that magic spell, hard enough that her lips curled in a smile that became part of their kiss. The little one's movements were such an instinctive, natural part of Kelly now that her response was invariably feeling a smile come from the inside out. Mac felt the baby move, too. Glued this close, even with all their coats and sweaters, he couldn't have missed it. His head shot up.

"What on earth...that was junior?"

"Uh-huh." She still had that smile. Sharing the baby with him only felt like more magic, just not quite of that same hot tempestuous brand.

And Mac smiled back at her for one precious, poignant second...until his expression suddenly seemed to freeze. He jolted back a step and dropped his hands as if he'd been handling hot potatoes. "What the hell are we doing, Kelly?"

"Necking on the front porch like a couple of teenagers?"

"Like a couple of people who've lost their minds, more like. Here you're pregnant and it's freezing cold out here..." He sucked in a breath. Guilt stained his face with color. "And the problem isn't the temperature. Kel, I'm sorry. I don't know what I was thinking of—"

Her mind was still operating on stun-power, her pulse still charging from the way he'd been with her moments before. But she told herself to get a fast grip, because some instinct warned her that however she handled this really mattered. "It's okay. There's nothing to be sorry for," she said gently.

"Not on your part. But I didn't mean to—"

She straightened his coat lapel. "Neither of us meant that to happen. But it did. So we both gave in to an impulse.

So we both needed to hold on to someone else for a moment. Does that sound like a crime to you?''

"Of course not, but—"

"I started this, not you. And I honestly didn't mean to start anything...awkward, Mac. We both seemed really sure that sexual feelings would never be a problem in this unusual relationship of ours. But I grew up on daily doses of hugs and kisses and a ton of affection. My mom used to say that no one should have to survive a day without a hug. And I realize you may not want that kind of thing. From me. So I'll try to be careful, but I admit that being pregnant has made me even more emotional, so I just can't promise I won't accidentally touch you. If you're going to be offended—"

"Kelly, nothing you could do would offend me," Mac said swiftly.

His lips were still parted to say something else, but she interrupted before he could. "Good. That's a worry off my mind. Like you said, we can make our own rules for this relationship. Nothing's a problem if we just honestly talk it out—and I'm headed in, Mac. In fact, I think I'm headed straight upstairs for a warm bath and bed. I'm really beat."

As they walked in the house and stashed their coats, she tried to keep up an easy patter, thanking him for dinner, for coming to the class, making some natural small talk about his travels and how his business had gone. He answered in half sentences, not clipping her off but just sounding distracted. But she felt his eyes on her as she climbed the stairs.

Her heart was clanging like a heavy fire engine bell until she turned the corner upstairs out of his sight.

Mac didn't want her. She'd known that from day one. And the last thing she'd ever intended was to wake that sleeping tiger, because she never wanted him to know how attracted she was. Still, she refused to regret that embrace.

Mac had been incomparably good to her. She needed to bring him something in the relationship. Not sex. Not behavior that would embarrass him. But her husband's whole life was hounded with responsibilities that never quit. He needed to laugh. To loosen up. To be around someone who didn't call him Mr. Fortune and wasn't expecting something from him all the time.

It wouldn't kill him to suffer through a hug now and then.

As long as she didn't do anything crazy like fall in love with him, Kelly didn't think there was a lick of harm.

Five

"No, don't waste your time digging for personal scandal—you know I hate that kind of thing. I couldn't care less if he were a cross-dresser. That's not my business—and his business life is all I'm interested in. What I want is the most complete financial dossier you can put together on Gray McGuire. Preferably by yesterday." When Mac heard knuckles rap on his office door, he twisted around with the phone still tucked to his ear. He motioned for his cousin Jack to come in. "Call me as soon as you've got anything, even if it's at home, okay? And thanks, Sterling."

By the time Mac hung up from talking with the corporate attorney, his cousin had closed the door—a sure sign there was trouble—and was prowling the teak-and-leather office as if he were too restless to sit down. At thirty-one, Jack Fortune was young to be vice president of marketing, but Mac had watched him grow and thrive in the role. Usually they touched base daily, but Mac's piled-high desk was testimony to what few hours he'd been in the office this whole last week.

Truth to tell, he wasn't denting the crisis pile very fast. Kelly was on his mind more than work. But Jack wouldn't have stopped if there weren't a problem, and Mac threw out a business question as he tried to gauge his cousin's mood. "Any chance you found out anything more about Gray McGuire?"

"I put out some feelers, but I didn't hear back anything that you haven't already heard. He's CEO of McGuire Industries. He does computer-related stuff—nothing in common with our business—so I don't have a clue why he'd be trying to buy up stock in Stuart Fortune's Knight Star Systems. You still think he's trying to pull off a takeover?"

"I don't think. I know. But I just can't make sense of it. McGuire's gone at this like he has a vendetta—watching, waiting for the company to hit a rough patch and then pouncing to take advantage. But we're no competition to him. I can't find any connection at all. Still, we've got good people working on it. Something'll surface." Mac dropped that subject. Talking business obviously wasn't engaging his cousin's attention. He watched Jack throw himself in the saddle leather chair across from the desk, then lurch right back up to repace the office like an antsy cat. "What's on your mind?"

Jack pointed to his blond head. "You see this gray hair? It's all caused by women."

Offhand, Mac didn't see a single gray hair, but he cocked a foot on his desk with an empathetic grin. "If you came to ask my advice on women, you're out of luck. I just found myself married to one. As far as I can tell, this is a shock to the system on a par with being suddenly hit with a tornado."

That brought a chuckle. Jack relaxed enough to lean against the tall teak credenza. "And that reminds me—I'm supposed to grill you. The whole family expects me to give you the third degree on how it's going with the new bride."

"So tell them it's going fine. I admit I'm still a husband-in-training, but Kelly's a sweetheart."

"That's the best you can do? That's not even an appetizer for the women in the family. They want details. They want dirt. Preferably they want juicy details about your sex life."

"Afraid they'll have to go hungry. They should know by now I don't participate in one of those gossip-feeding frenzies," Mac said dryly. He suspected that Jack might be as curious as the rest—or these questions wouldn't have come up—but his cousin at least respected that Mac just wasn't one to confide about his personal life. A good thing, because Mac wasn't about to tell anyone that he was petrified of his new bride.

From nowhere, unbidden, unwanted, memories from that starlit night a week ago seeped into his mind...the look of Kelly's red mouth, swollen from his kisses, the never-expected fire of desire in her eyes, the stupid, crazy feeling of longing and need that had somehow snipered all his common sense.

Even seven days later, guilt still made his stomach muscles clench. My God, she was almost eight-months pregnant and had been through nonstop stress, and he'd come on to her like a horny teenage boy. He'd spun that memory in his mind a dozen times and still couldn't explain or excuse his response to her...and worse yet, that hadn't been the end of it. Thinking of all the things Kelly had done to him over this past week made him instinctively pat his shirt pocket for antacids. Hell, he was fresh out. And his cousin had started pacing the office again. "I can't believe you've got a woman problem, Jack. I thought you swore off that whole half of the human species after your divorce."

"I did, I did. Unfortunately, taking up a nice, safe celibate lifestyle didn't make Sandra disappear. She called me this morning. She's thinking about getting married again."

"So where's the problem? She can make some other guy's life hell instead of bugging you."

"That part sounds fine. But she's sabotaged every time I'm supposed to get Lilly. Three years old and my daughter barely knows me. And if Sandra marries again I'm afraid she'll try to make it that much harder."

Mac paused. "Money always talked to her before."

"Yes, greed works. I've been down that bribery road before, no reason I can't try it again." Jack sighed. "It just bites my pride and sense of ethics both—she thinks she wins every time I give her money. And what bugs me the most is what the whole mess says about my judgment in women—that I ever picked her for a wife, much less for the mother of my daughter."

"I think sometimes it's pretty hard to tell what's in a package from the way it's wrapped."

They talked life and business for a few more minutes, but when Jack finally left, Mac suddenly felt more restless than his cousin. He pushed out of his office chair and hiked over to the wall of windows. Below, Minneapolis had turned winter-gloomy. The pretty holiday trimmings were gone, the snow turned old and crusty gray, traffic snarling like normal again. Mac looked, but all he saw in his mind's eye was Kelly. She was "wrapped" in such a normal package. The silky-fine blond hair, the soft blue eyes, the sunshine smiles...she was cute; she was real; she was attractive in entirely her own way. But there was nothing in her appearance to warn a man that she was more dangerous than a firecracker in a closed room.

One week of marriage and his nerves were in shreds. It was that Hugging Thing, Mac thought morosely.

Touching her was never supposed to be a problem. For damn sure, he never thought sex would be. Her being in love with his brother should have guaranteed his wiltability, no matter how attractive he found her—and yeah, Kelly had told him several times now that she would never have married Chad. But what Mac really heard were hurt feelings. However real that hurt, it didn't mean that her love had died, and her confessed inexperience only affirmed for Mac that Kelly was never a woman to sleep with a man lightly.

Only she'd brought up that hugging business—and she'd made it sound as if she'd grown up so used to physical affection that she couldn't survive without her daily hug quota. Mac never remotely assumed she was counting on him for a hug source—that wouldn't even make sense with their particular relationship—but all week long, all this complicated stuff kept happening. Like this morning, she'd been laughing and joking her way through an insane breakfast of pickles and cereal. Then she'd burned some toast—like who cared?—only suddenly her eyes were welling with these horrible, big, fat tears.

A few days before that, they'd had a couple of little electronic crises. Damned if he knew how she'd crashed a hard drive and sabotaged two VCRs in a single day, but Mac had always believed in facing reality. Kelly was an electronic nimwit—that was clearly going to be their reality—so he'd come home with another VCR and a personal computer for her. Now how on earth was he supposed to know that would make her cry again?

And she did other things. Weird things. Like make him a mess of spareribs and a rhubarb pie, when his own family didn't know those were his favorites. Like bringing him home a box of malted milk chocolates—which he hadn't been addicted to since he was a kid—and for no reason. She hung up his coats and tuned to the stock market report over breakfast and kept the kitchen stashed with oatmeal-raisin cookies. And then there was the afternoon she'd so gravely tried to listen to him about how to work the security system, and still somehow managed to set off every alarm on the whole property....

Mac clawed a hand through his hair. None of those circumstances precisely required a hug to fix them, only when she reached out her arms, he never felt he had a choice. She was pregnant and she'd had all this stress. He couldn't make her feel rejected. He couldn't upset her.

He never thought marriage was easy—hell, he hadn't escaped rings all these years because he had any illusions on that score—but Kelly was supposed to be different. Even before proposing marriage, his role in her life had been mirror-clear to him. He had a job—to keep her safe. He needed to turn around the mess his brother had made, and make both Kelly and the baby's life secure. That was a job he was uniquely qualified to do. His whole life, he'd been a problem-solver, not a problem-causer.

He didn't fail people. Ever.

Only he'd never expected this confounded hug thing to come up. He'd never expected that she'd want to touch him, much less that he'd respond to her as if she were the only woman in the entire universe who had ever mattered. Hell. The damn woman was becoming the sunshine of his life.

Mac squeezed his eyes closed, thinking that he had an outstanding reason not to go home until late tonight. The family had saved him by putting together a surprise for Kelly, so he had some extra hours to make sure he worked this out in his head before seeing her again.

But Mac didn't really need that time. He knew exactly what had to be. Kelly needed to be able to trust him. She needed to know that she could count on him. Her getting under his emotional skin only made it more imperative that he not fail her in the things that mattered. Which meant— cut-and-dried—that he needed to keep his hands off her.

Mac knew what was right.

He just had to do it.

Kelly pushed back her coat sleeve to glance at her watch. "Benz, we really need to get home. I appreciate your taking the time to show me around the area, but—"

"Yeah, I didn't want you getting lost if you took off on your own sometime. Lots of twists and turns in this neck of the woods."

Kelly started to respond, then fretfully twisted her watch-band instead. Something strange was going on. She just couldn't figure out what it was. They'd left the house right after lunch, because Benz asked for her help picking out a birthday present for Martha. That was fine, only after shopping he'd then gotten the idea she should familiarize herself with the neighborhood. And that was also fine, except that Benz had been cruising at twenty-five miles an hour on back roads with nothing but woods and more woods for ages now.

"It's past four," she ventured again. "The thing is, I don't know what time Mac's coming home from the office—"

"Believe me, he won't be home this early. Not tonight."

"How come you're so sure of that?"

"I just know, that's all." Benz shot her a mysterious smile.

Benz just wasn't a man to pull off a mysterious smile. He was obviously trying to hide something from her, but they finally seemed to be on the road headed home. She could wait to hear what his surprise was. Her mind was on Mac.

He'd come home tired, she suspected. And there'd be no one to unplug the phones and make him put his feet up for a few minutes if she weren't there. After living with him for a week, the handwriting was on the wall. Calls came in at all hours of the day and night. Some were family, some business, but neither contingent seemed to appreciate that Mac had a life and was entitled to some downtime.

As the tall gates came into view, Kelly dove in her purse for a brush and fresh lipstick. Maybe their marriage was still new, but she'd already figured out she didn't want to be one of his burdens. Too many people called Mac with problems. Too many people expected him to leap in and rescue them from a tough problem, and it grated like a fingernail on a chalkboard that she was one of them. He never acted annoyed to be stuck with a pregnant stranger who accidentally destroyed all his electronic equipment. In point of fact, he was so ceaselessly considerate and kind that he was driving her half crazy.

But Kelly figured she could fix that. She was still struggling to find a place in his life—not an intrusive place, not to be in his way. She hadn't and didn't expect Mac to love her. And she was well aware that Mac was uncomfortable with her impulsive hugs—but he was getting used to them, she thought. The darn man needed hugs. He needed someone he felt free to be downright crabby with. He needed someone, for God's sake, who wasn't always asking or expecting something from him.

Never. Never had she met a man more worth loving or who had so many special loving qualities—not, Kelly assured herself, that she was falling for him. Mac never had to know that these simple physical gestures were increasingly turning her knees to jelly. She'd just find some way to deal with that. This wasn't about her. It was about finding a way to make this relationship good for Mac, not just for her, and it was so obvious that he needed...but abruptly her thoughts were interrupted when the house came into view.

"Okay, what's going on?" she demanded to Benz.

"Why, nothing, honey."

"The house is all lit up like a Christmas tree. And you know how zealous y'all are about security, yet I can see the front door's ajar—"

"Well, there's probably a good reason Martha left the door open. Martha probably just left a few seconds ago, and she knew we were overdue. But if Mac wasn't home yet, she wouldn't want you coming into a dark house, and she knows what a hard time you have with the security system."

"Uh-huh. Sounds like bologna to me, but it's obvious I'm not going to get a straight answer out of you, so we'll just settle this tomorrow." Kelly smacked his cheek good-bye, then heaved out of the car and waddled to the front door. She'd just stepped in and kicked off her right boot when a chorus of feminine voices suddenly yelled, "Surprise!"

She was half braced for something, and Benz wouldn't have been so happily playing around if the "something" had been a problem. Still, she'd never expected anything like a surprise baby shower. Familiar faces swarmed in front of her. Her friend Mollie. Kate. Renee. Chloe, Mac's sister, dressed so typically in a flamboyant purple that matched her incredible violet eyes. Amanda Corbain, who worked in marketing with Mac's cousin Jack, and had become a wonderful friend at work. Marie, Mac's aunt, who did the matriarchal thing on her side of the family the way Kate did with her side of the clan.

Red faced and laughing, Kelly tried to express thanks as the group descended on her. The next couple of hours were a fast ride. The Fortunes never did anything halfway. A buffet feast had been catered in, with an ice sculpture for a centerpiece in the shape of a Pooh bear, and the presents crowding Mac's great room were beyond generous—a crib, high chair, stroller, car seat and heaven knew, toys ranging from sterling-silver rattles to a four-foot white teddy bear.

After that came gifts for the mom—a day at the spa, luxury creams for stretch marks, lingerie for when she got her figure back that made her blush.

Kelly felt so overwhelmed that she felt tears well a couple of times, which only pleased her shower givers no end. By the time the gifts were all opened, the house looked destroyed. Wrapping paper and debris littered every surface. At least one cider and coffee had spilled. Plates cluttered the tables. And the women had all gotten fresh drinks and settled down to talk.

"I don't know how to thank you all. I never expected anything like this," Kelly said emotionally.

"Nonsense, dear, you're family now." Kate's eyes crinkled in a smile. "And we grilled Mac so we'd know what colors you wanted to put in the nursery—"

"He also filled us in on our addition to teddy bears," Amanda teased.

"I want credit for the lingerie ideas." Marie sighed. Mac's Aunt Marie was the matriarch on one side of the Fortune family—but a little vintage only sharpened the lively sparkle in her eyes. "You young girls dress way too much in jeans. I realize I'm getting older, but I don't think this younger generation has a clue how to keep a marriage together. A little black lace and candlelight never hurt a thing."

The women hooted. "I guess we know why Stuart never strayed all those years, huh, Marie?"

"Heavens, no. Stuart wouldn't stray because he knows perfectly well I'd murder him if he tried," Marie said dryly.

In the midst of all the laughter, Kelly saw Mollie suddenly turn pale and leave the room. Concerned, Kelly started to rise to go after her friend, but just then Mac's sister waved her hands to get the group's attention.

"Well, while we're talking about sex and what it takes to keep a marriage together, it seems a pretty good time to

make an announcement.'' Chloe, curled up in the corner of
the pink couch, and humorously popped a ribbon on her
head. ''Before Mason and I turn this into the longest en-
gagement in history, we finally got around to setting a date.
The marriage is on for November.''

The whole group exuberantly congratulated her, but
Kelly couldn't help but notice that everyone seemed happier than Chloe. ''What made you suddenly decide to set
the date?''

''I dunno. It just seemed time. At the rate we've been
moving, we could have been engaged forever.''

''Which might be best if you're not sure,'' Kate said
shrewdly.

''I'm dead sure. I've been crazy about that man from the
day I met him. Mason's just…well, on some things, he's
hard to pin down. Typical man, huh?'' Chloe's words were
light, but her tone so unexpectedly serious that the others
fell silent, as if sensing there was a problem she wasn't
saying. Swiftly Chloe grinned and waved her hands in a
dismissive gesture. ''And enough on that. Let's turn the
attention back on Kelly. I want to hear how she's surviving
marriage to my big brother—does he or doesn't he take off
those starched shirts when the lights go out?''

''Honestly, Chloe, you don't have to be so blunt,'' Marie
scolded.

''Aw, come on. You're all wondering the same thing.
We all know about the baby, Kel, but there always had to
be more to this. Mac's been allergic to marriage forever.
He never let a woman get close. Hells bells, he never let
any of the family all that close, either. None of us could
ever get him to talk.''

''Like his cousin Jack,'' Amanda said irritably. ''I work
with that man every day and still can't get a personal word
out of him.''

''That's different, though. Jack only turned quiet after

the divorce. Mac's never been burned by anyone—at least that he's told family, even me." Chloe turned to Kelly. "We all love him, Kel. I don't know any member of the family that he hasn't come through for sometime. So maybe we do pry a little far, but it's because we want him to be happy. We want you to be happy, too. We wouldn't be asking questions if we didn't care."

They could hire out as an inquisition team, Kelly thought. The nosy, poking questions kept coming, and so did some astounding advice on how she should handle Mac. Another hour passed, yet no one made a move to leave. For a few minutes she escaped to the bathroom, but en route through the kitchen, she found Mollie, neck deep in plastic bags and paper plates. "Hey, you. Kate said the catering service would show up in the morning to clean up. You don't have to do that."

"You know me. I can't sit," Mollie said with a grin.

Kelly studied her friend. "Yeah, I know you. And the way you disappeared, I was afraid you were ill or something was wrong—"

"No, no, I'm fine."

Kelly poured a short glass of milk as an excuse to linger. Mac and her new marriage had dominated her whole life, but she hadn't meant to neglect her old friend, and Mollie didn't look remotely "fine." Her pale skin was always striking against her vibrant red hair, but tonight her complexion looked paper-white. The five year age difference had made them unlikely friends growing up, but they practically lived next door, and both their moms were single parents. Because Mollie's mother worked long hours running a flower shop, Kelly often baby-sat or just hung around so Mol wouldn't be alone. But the thing was, she'd always had a protective older sister feeling for her friend, and now was no different. "Something's bothering you."

"Yeah, there is." Mollie admitted it, but then hesitated.

"It's just something personal I'm trying to work out, Kel. I'm not trying to be secretive. I just want to work through it on my own before talking about it."

Kelly could understand that, but her friend's choice of silence only made the problem sound bigger and more worrisome. "Is this something related to why you left in the middle of the reception? You never really said, Mol, and I was worried something had happened then, too. I was hoping you'd make a ton of good contacts to get your wedding-planner business going—"

"And it worked out great that way," Mollie assured her, but she averted her eyes. "And the reason I left...well, it was losing Mom so recently. It all just got to me, that she'd never see me married, never know I was finally really putting my business together, either. I just had a big, lousy attack of sadness, that's all. But by the time I came back inside, you and Mac were gone..." Swiftly she changed the subject. "Whew, can those women dish out the third degree or what? I could hear some of the questions they were asking you from here."

"I don't think there was a shy Fortune ever born, but I know them all now. They're all coming from caring."

"Yeah, I can see that. But man, are they nosy." Mollie hesitated. "And you weren't answering any of their questions, but there's only you and me here now. And I know how busy you've been, but you haven't told me one thing about how you two really got together. I mean, do you love him? Does he love you? How do both of you feel about this baby being his brother's?"

More questions. And Kelly loved her friend, had come to love many of the Fortune women as if they were real family, too. But she wasn't willing to discuss her relationship with Mac with anyone. Her feelings were both too private and too confused. And although she was increasingly scared that she was falling dangerously in love with him, it struck her sense of irony that he was one person in the universe she really wanted to be with. Mac never pushed or pressured her about anything. There was a time she'd never dreamed she could be comfortable with the formidable Mackenzie Fortune, but he'd never been formidable with her. She could be herself with him. The only thing she had to guard against were those loving feelings, but everything else—her nurturing nature and emotional impulsiveness, every flaw and foible right down to her hopelessness near anything electronic—Mac had been more accepting of her than she'd ever been of herself.

She rejoined the party, pulling Mollie back into the group with her, laughing and chatting with the women no different than before. They told her Mac had orders to stay away and leave them to their "girl fest." Still, the instant she heard the click of the front door around eight, the muffled sound was enough to make her spring to her feet and fly for the door. She was vaguely aware that the women abruptly quit talking. She wasn't thinking about them; she was just thinking how glad she was to see him. And when Mac stomped in, his shoulders and head sprinkled with a fresh layer of snow, it seemed the most natural thing on earth to throw her arms around him.

Six

Mac had explicit orders from the women not to show up at this shower shindig until after nine. Originally he thought he'd be thrilled to comply. He ordered some fast food, looking forward to the quiet hours after the employees had gone home to make a serious dent in his overflowing desk. Only he couldn't seem to concentrate on work. He kept worrying how it was going for Kelly.

He had no doubt the all-female party would be great fun for her, but her pregnancy was the thing. Every day she got closer to term, the faster she tired out. And when she got tired, a puff of wind could make her tearful. Mac's women kin were another worry—he loved them; they were family, but they did have a teensy tendency to be unilaterally domineering. He just figured it would be a good idea for him to come home early, tiptoe in, sneak a peek to make sure it was all going okay for her and then disappear upstairs until the shower thing was all over.

That was the new plan, and Mac could have sworn he was quieter than a guilty teenager when he opened the front door. The women had all hid their cars beyond the garage, so Kelly wouldn't see them, and he parked even further back to give them turnaround room in the driveway, but by then it was snowing in buckets. Even in that short walk to the door, his cheeks were burning from the fierce wind and snow already soaking his hair and coat...and suddenly there she was, hurtling around the corner with her arms outstretched. "Mac! You're home!"

He barely had a second to brace. He should have. When his bride got it in her head that she wanted a hug, Mac already knew well that she wasn't one to wait around until next Tuesday to think it over. Faster than a jet-propelled missile, she exuberantly flew into his arms, tummy first, and suddenly she was snuggled against the length of him.

That suddenly, he was in trouble.

After the razor-blast of frigid night air, she felt warmer than firelight, softer than sunshine. She smelled so good; she felt so good that his arms instinctively tightened around her. He was hard in two seconds flat—and Mac had been trying to tell himself all week that was a justifiable biological response for a man who'd been celibate too long. Only he'd been celibate for stretches before and never once responded to any other woman the way he did Kelly.

It was like a chocoholic who caught a whiff of the finest chocolate. He was becoming addicted. He had no idea where the craving first came from, but that wreath of a welcoming smile—no one had ever been glad to see Mac, not like her, not like she was just "happy." That he was in her universe. She liked being with him—for no reason in hell that he could tell—but it sucker-punched his emotions every time. Her smiles, her skin, those butter-soft blue eyes, the feel of her slim-boned shoulders in his arms and the baby tucked between them...

He found his mouth pressing into her hair before he could stop it. She must have felt that kiss, because she suddenly lifted her head. Warning sirens screeched in his mind. She searched his face, and damned if he knew what she saw, but as if he'd said "please," she surged up on tiptoe and kissed him, her lips tremulous and vibrant and satin-smooth.

It wasn't the first time electric awareness had sparked between them like a power surge. It wasn't the first time his mind had fast-rolled a fantasy of carrying her off to bed and to hell with the consequences. Her fingers clenched at the back of his head and her lips moved against his, softly, shyly, like a rosebud opening for a drink of sunlight. He'd known women, a ton of women, a ton of skilled and erotically sophisticated women who had never once provoked him to murder and mayhem. It was something about Kelly that bewitched him. He could taste her vulnerability. He could taste the invitation in the way she kissed him. He could imagine all that warmth, wrapped around him, could imagine all that exuberance and giving and all that passion for life, just for him.

A dozen times Mac had reminded himself that his brother was in this picture and he'd be a fool to forget that. He hadn't forgotten. It was just that she was so increasingly hard to let go of. If the crazy magic she generated wasn't real, it felt perfectly, painfully, treasuringly real when she was in his arms and kissing him back as if nothing and no one mattered but the two of them.

Eventually his conscience pierced through all those greedy emotions and finally surfaced. Honor mattered. Not just to him, but for her. Kelly needed him. This whole marriage had been put together because Kelly needed a man she could trust And the more he came to care for her, the more it mattered to Mac that he couldn't, wouldn't, fail her.

So he severed the kiss slowly, not loosening his arms too far, not wanting her to feel rejected or worried about trusting him. And he smiled, as if desire wasn't biting at his nerves with sharp teeth, as if need weren't still thrumming in his veins in a hot rush of blood. And his smile became real after a moment. This morning he'd left her looking so crisp and put-together in a pale blue maternity dress. Now, though, her collar was askew, a ribbon dangling from her shoulder, and her hair looked wildly tumbled, silk-fine strands flying every which way. "I take it you've been having a terrific time at the shower?"

"Oh, Mac, I couldn't wait for you to get home so I could tell you. You wouldn't believe—"

She bubbled over with the details, giving him another few seconds to gather his wits—and his conscience—and suck up that need for her. But he was just plucking the ribbon from her shoulder when he suddenly realized they weren't alone.

It looked like the entire shower of women was standing in the doorway, as silent as statues, all staring at his arms around Kelly and grinning at him like female goons.

He never had to move from the front door, because the crowd cleared out faster than a marine bivouac. He delivered coats and extensive thanks, accepted cheek pats and mauling from his female relatives and more of those allknowing female smiles.

When the last one left, he ambled with Kelly into the living room. One glance and he stopped dead. "Holy cow."

She laughed. "Pretty petrifying mess, huh? But we don't have to worry about it. Your aunts said it was part of the catering service deal to come back in the morning and clean up."

"You sure it wouldn't just be easier to have the place

condemned and move? I'm almost positive we have insurance for natural disasters like this.''

She chuckled again, and excitedly dragged him around for a tour of all the presents. It took a while. Eventually he settled in the corner of the pink couch with his feet up—it had been a killer long day, and somebody needed to enjoy the big thick cushions of the couch. Kelly hadn't sat in the thing since he'd moved it in here. She said it ruined his decor. Mac contended that it was the most comfortable piece of furniture either of them owned. So far that was an unsolved argument, but at that moment, he primarily crashed to encourage her to get off her feet, too. He knew she had to be tired. "You're telling me one small, eight-pound baby has to have approximately three hundred pounds of stuff just to survive a basic day?"

"I was informed that we hadn't even started. Although I can't imagine anything they didn't think of. You really do have an incredibly wonderful family.'' He should have known she was still too revved up to settle down. After dancing through the boxes and papers again, she hunched over the high chair carton. An instruction sheet emerged. Followed by terrifying little bags of screws and spare parts. "The family has some funny ideas about you, though."

"Funny ideas? Like what?"

"I got a lot of advice. On your likes and dislikes. How to keep you happy. They think you have a temper, Mac."

"Uh, Tiny. I do." A couple of wooden legs emerged from the carton. The more parts showed up, the more his throat went dry. "You're not planning on putting that together at this minute, are you?"

"Sure. It says, 'Easy To Assemble.' But we'll need both a regular and a Phillips head screwdriver—you sit, I know where everything is." She jogged to the kitchen, came back juggling tools and two glass mugs of mulled cider. "And I'm not through telling you all your family's advice. Chloe informed me that it was important for me to start doing some serious entertaining. Your sister says you have to do all kinds of social things for the company, and any woman in your life had better clue in to that ambitious, social kind of thing.''

Mac's jaw almost dropped. "I hope you weren't listening. I've never done black tie by choice in my entire life. I hate big political social gatherings like that with a passion.''

"That's what I thought." She was starting to wave those screwdrivers around like lethal weapons. "I found it pretty amazing. That none of them know you like to tromp around the woods. Cut your own firewood. Ski. That you love to read history. Most of the newlywed advice I got was related to joining you in the social limelight, but then there was your aunt Marie.''

"Yeah?" Hell. He lurched off the couch, hunkered down next to her, and grabbed the instruction sheet. He couldn't just sit there while she was working on the high chair by herself. That he didn't know a screwdriver from a wrench wasn't remotely relevant. Putting stuff together was man's work. "So what'd Aunt Marie have to say?"

"She told me the way to keep you happy was lots of sex. Mac, don't lose those nuts—nothing too kinky, she said. She didn't figure you'd go for blindfolds and leather. I should just stick with the basics, but make sure you got action on a regular basis…well, I'll be darned, is that a blush climbing your neck?''

"Picturing my aunt Marie discussing blindfolds and kinky sex is enough to make a monk blush," Mac muttered dryly. He hefted a strangely shaped piece of wood and tried to identify what it was from the instruction sheet—at least until Kelly tactfully removed it from his hands. Seconds later she was screwing that strange-shaped piece into another strange-shaped piece.

"Well...since you and I don't exactly have that kind of relationship, whether you prefer blindfolds or leather isn't exactly a worry. But in my personal opinion, I'm guessing you could get more than a little wild and inventive once the lights were out, Mr. Fortune."

Mac scrubbed a hand over his face. Something was brewing in those innocent blue eyes of hers. He remembered—with painful clarity—encouraging Kelly to believe she could be bluntly honest with him. And she was plenty honest, but never so blunt that she'd volunteered to tease him about sex before—much less following that intimate little encounter in the hallway that still had his hormones scrabbling with his sanity. "Did they spike your punch at this shower?" he asked suspiciously.

"Mac! I'm pregnant! In fact, all the other women had a glass of wine except for me...now just hold those legs steady for me, would you? Anyway, there's a reason I'm telling you about all their advice."

"What?" he asked warily.

"It worries me. That your family doesn't know you at all."

"Offhand, I'd say it'd be damn weird if the women in my family knew about my sexual preferences." His dry tone was an effort to coax a grin, but suddenly she'd turned real serious.

"I'm not talking about sex. I'm talking about love. Your family would never have bugged me with so many prying questions or advice if they didn't love you to bits, or care about your being happy. And from what I gather, you're the first one they turn to in a time of trouble, and you've been there for them. A zillion times. But they don't seem to know you at all. I don't get it. Who's there for you when the chips go down?"

She did that all the time. Confuse him. Ask confounding questions that nobody ever asked him. He never knew what she wanted him to say. "I'm a grown-up. If my chips go down, I fix the problem. I don't expect anyone to run around rescuing me."

Her eyes turned luminous with compassion. She pushed the half-finished high chair aside, as if she'd never really been concentrating on it anyway. "Everyone needs rescuing sometimes. And you're so good to people, but somehow your family's got this idea that you come through every time. Mac, no one can always do that. There has to be someone you're not afraid to confess a goof to. Someone who can help you know the world won't end if you make a mistake."

Mac shifted edgily. Kelly's perception of his family was right on the money, but he'd always been perfectly fine with his problem-fixing role in the clan. He'd never been conscious of loneliness, until his bride started bringing up all this kind of emotional junk. He'd never missed other people being close. Until her. Until he started missing her when she wasn't around—the way her baby-fine hair flew around her face. The way her soft eyes seemed to look right inside him when she brought up this kind of emotional stuff. The way she intently listened, the dot of freckles on her nose, those slim long legs…

When he realized his gaze was traveling down the highway of her body parts—again—he pulled himself up short. Time to change the subject. And since she seemed determined to wander around some dicey topics in this conversation, he figured it was as good a time as any to confront a tough one. "I think the family'll quit bugging you with all that embarrassing advice after tonight."

Her eyebrows arched in question. "Why do you think they'll quit?"

"Because they saw you in my arms, Tiny. God knows, there's no shortage of ruthlessness in my family—but that's business. Every one of them is a sucker for love, which is what they thought they were seeing."

There now. It was her turn to flush and look edgily unnerved. "Mac, I didn't hug you or do anything else to fake them out. I didn't realize they were watching. I was just excited when you came in, I couldn't wait to tell you about everything—"

"I never thought you were doing anything manipulative, Kel. But I do think we've got a building problem that needs talking out." He hesitated. "You have to know there's chemistry between us. And it's not going away. Affection is one thing, but you're not hugging me like a brother. And I'm sure as hell not hugging you back like you were my sister."

She went still, her gaze studying his face. He remembered when she used to skitter around him in the office, as if he intimidated or made her uncomfortable. For damn sure he never wanted to go back to those days, but at least he'd known what she was thinking then. "Would you rather I made sure not to touch you?" she asked carefully.

"No."

Her eyes never budged from his. "Are you telling me you want nothing to do with this chemistry?"

"No," he said again, and then irritably rubbed the back of his neck. "I just don't think it's a good idea to pretend it isn't there. You can't solve a problem you're not willing to face. I don't think either of us were expecting this particular little dragon…and we'd both better be honest about where we think this relationship is going."

"All right," she said slowly. "From the beginning you said we could create this marriage by our own rules. By whatever worked for us. And it seems to me that's exactly what we're doing, Mac. Exploring. Each other." She hesitated. "Do you think it'd be such a terrible idea if we ended up physically close?"

Now how had he ended up in the hot seat again? It was her feelings Mac wanted to understand, not his. Faster than a sniper's bullet, images of making love with her flooded his mind—but what "he" wanted had nothing to do with this. He rubbed the back of his neck. Again. "What I think is that making love complicates a relationship—and that's not a complication you volunteered for when we first made this alliance. I don't want you worried that you can't trust me. I don't want something starting accidentally and ending up with something you regret. I'm also watching you get more and more physically uncomfortable the closer you get to term. So I'm not for ignoring the attraction as if it didn't exist. But I'm suggesting we table it until after the baby's born."

He had no idea how she'd respond, but he wasn't expecting a suddenly loosening of her shoulder muscles and a soft, easy smile. "There's no question about my trusting you, Mac. And okay—that sounds like a plan to me. As long as you're not going to deny me my daily quota of hugs—"

He felt relieved they were back to lightweight teasing. "Hugs are still in the program, Tiny."

"Well…if we've got all that straight, I have to say I'm downright groggy tired. I'm going to take the baby and me off to bed." She leaned over, pressed her lips to his forehead before he could guess she intended to do it, then awkwardly climbed to her feet. Halfway to the door, she called back, "Um, Mac?"

"What?"

"Don't even think about reaching for that screwdriver."

"I beg your pardon?" She hadn't even turned around to see what his hand was or wasn't reaching for.

"I'll finish the high chair in the morning. It's just a tiny bit obvious that you don't know an O ring from a washer.

Actually it's a relief to know you're a mechanical klutz. It makes up for me being such a klutz with electronic stuff.''

His vocal chords were primed to defend his macho mechanical abilities, but she'd already turned the corner out of sight. Mac leaned back and tossed down the screwdriver. God knew how many legs the high chair would have ended up with if he'd tried finishing the assembly job.

Every lamp and light was on in the room, cheerily illuminating the wall-to-wall ribbons and bows and boxes. Yet it was funny, how all the life disappeared once Kelly left. His mood seemed to drop like a deflating balloon.

Still, Mac shagged a hand through his hair, thinking at least that touchy little talk had gone well. He didn't understand her, but that wasn't news. Actually she seemed to confound him more each day—but that wasn't news, either.

She hadn't directly said she wanted to sleep with him, but Mac would have self-destructed long before the age of thirty-eight if he couldn't recognize dynamite by now. The explosive potential was there. He was no stranger to passion, but no woman had ever responded to simple kisses, basic touches, with the open, giving, heart-blind passion as she did. She wanted him. And he damn well wanted her back—like a craving in his blood and a hot claw around his heart—except that he was too worried about the "why." Maybe she felt gratitude or as if she owed him something. Maybe living together had created a propinquity problem. Maybe she was at such a vulnerable time in the pregnancy that her emotions were just wildly volatile—volatile enough to at least make her temporarily forget his brother.

Postponing any action until after the baby was born would give her breathing space to think, Mac believed. Weeks down the pike, she'd feel more secure. More on her feet. She could well decide she didn't need him for a damn thing—much less for sex. Waiting, giving her plenty of time to think, was simply the honorable thing to do.

Mac climbed to his feet, and started turning off lights. Minutes later he climbed the stairs for bed, thinking that he'd sworn to make this right for her and he damn well would.

But for the first and only time in his life, he thought: honor sucked.

In the middle of the night, Kelly was suddenly wakened by the baby's exuberant kicking—directly on her bladder. With her eyes barely open, she climbed out of bed with a hand instinctively stroking the taut skin of her abdomen. Her little one was a night owl. Kelly stumbled toward the door, so used to these nature calls in the middle of the night that she needed no light on to guide her down the hall to the bathroom.

She felt the thick cushioned carpet on her bare feet, the chill night drafts whispering around her nightgown, then the icy tile of the coral bathroom off the nursery. Still, she didn't mind her sleep interrupted. Somehow these predawn interruptions seemed a uniquely private time between her and the baby. The sensation of the little one growing inside her, moving all the time now, always invoked a precious feeling of wonder. The rush of huge, engulfing love she felt for the baby was like nothing else.

She'd never doubted wanting the little one. Even when she first discovered she was pregnant—knowing how disappointed her mother would have been at her morals, knowing Chad had disappeared and she'd been foolish to believe he loved her—her wanting the baby had never been a question. If she'd known how to contact Chad, she would have tried, but only because it seemed wrong not to inform him. He'd been vocal about not wanting children. She knew she was alone. She knew exactly how hard it was to be a single parent from her own mother's struggles. But her mom had also taught her about courage and strength, and Kelly had never felt deprived of love, could feel the power of that love for her baby from the start. She'd felt guilt over the poor choices she'd made, but never, never, even an ounce of regret.

Yet in the pitch-black bathroom with the numb-the-toes-cold tiles, one regret surfaced in her mind. She wished—suddenly, fiercely, painfully—that Mac were her baby's father.

The baby quit kicking and went back to sleep. She rinsed her hands, vaguely dried them on a towel and then stumbled back into the hall toward her bedroom. From nowhere in the dark she collided with something solid and hard and warm. Her forehead felt the spank of a chin. Her leg cracked against his unyielding shinbone.

And then Mac's hands reached out to gentle and steady her. His bark of a groggy chuckle sounded hoarse from sleepiness and pain both. "Hell. I figured this was one of your three o'clock potty runs, but I got up just to make sure you weren't sick or something. I didn't have in mind sending us both to the emergency room from the injuries of crashing together. You okay?"

She felt his knuckles brushing against her cheek, the gesture tender, soothing, as if he could feel if she were okay in the complete darkness. "I'm fine. Really, Mac."

"Okay. Sleep good, Tiny." His hands dropped. He really was still asleep, because she heard him careen off a wall as he aimed back for his bedroom.

And Kelly awakened like a slam then, thinking how hugely she'd lied. She wasn't fine. She wasn't remotely fine. Her stinging leg and throbbing forehead would recover in a few seconds. But she was in love with him and falling deeper every day.

He was so good to her. That was part of it, but it was

discovering Mac's secrets that was slowly, inexorably proving her undoing. It was watching him fumble with a screwdriver and pretend he knew what he was doing. It was watching him caretake and protect too damn many people—and God she didn't want to be one of those people ceaselessly counting on him—but he didn't seem to even know what a special, rare, giving man he was. It was seeing his aloneness. It was watching him give, so willingly, from that huge heart of his. It was knowing his addiction for oatmeal-raisin cookies. It was his shock when she did something for him. It was his instinctively getting up in the middle of the night to make sure she was okay.

How was she *not* supposed to love him?

As she curled up back in bed and snuggled deeply, darkly, under the covers, she reminded herself that he'd only married her from a sense of responsibility. And she'd only add to that feeling of responsibility if Mac knew she loved him.

She had to get tough. She had to stay quiet. She simply refused to hurt this man who had been so incredibly good to her.

Seven

Swiftly Kelly pushed open the gold-rimmed doors to the Fortune company lobby and charged toward the elevators. George, the security guard, had walked her in, but this late in the day—past six—she was hoping most of the employees had gone home. She hadn't been back inside the Fortune headquarters in a month now, and any other time she'd have loved to catch up with old friends. Tonight, though, she was not only in a hustle, but her ski parka and cranberry sweat suit and snowboots didn't exactly fit with the Fortune formal dress code. Particularly carrying a bulky satchel, Kelly figured she looked more like an aspiring bag lady than a corporate wife.

Well, there was no help for it. Glamour and women with submarine-size tummies just didn't go together, and with any luck, she wouldn't run into anyone except for Mac's secretary.

Luck was on her side. Once the elevators whooshed open

on Mac's floor, she didn't see a soul until she hiked into the outer office. Ellen immediately rose from her desk chair. Typically Mac's secretary was dressed with immaculate taste, a gray-and-taupe dress, her silvery hair twisted in an elegant bun—but her smile was warm and welcoming. Kelly never had to worry about putting on the dog for Ellen—she protected Mac better than a bulldog, which was all it had taken for the two women to become friends.

"Kelly! It's good to see you. I'll get Mr. Fortune right away—"

"No, no, I didn't come here to interrupt him. I just talked with him on the phone a couple hours ago, so I know he's tied up with meetings."

"Well, yes, he is. But if he knew you were here—"

"It's okay. I didn't come to see him. I just came to drop something off." She dropped the satchel on Ellen's desk. "I'm on my way to childbirth class—originally Mac had planned to go with me, but when I heard what a horrendous meeting schedule he had today, I told him to skip it. But since I was in town, anyway…well, you know how he is. He'll go for fast food if there's no time to catch a real dinner. And he'll likely pick Mexican, because he loves it—"

"And likely hot Mexican, because he likes that even more." Ellen's eyes were already twinkling. Maybe her style and manners were formal, but she and Kelly had the same certain insider information on the boss. "And then he'll be—"

"—Sick to his stomach and cranky. So I just brought him a dinner he could microwave." Kelly didn't mention there was another package in the satchel. Mac would find it, and Ellen didn't need to know.

They'd survived a month of marriage as of today. She thought Mac deserved a reward, but what to give him was the problem. Her heart wanted to put together a romantic dinner, but her heart was increasingly, stubbornly, dumb where Mac was concerned. An intelligent, eight-month-pregnant woman shouldn't have her mind on sex all the time—or on seducing a husband who didn't want to be seduced. Really, any gift of sentiment or expense or that hinted of romantic was only likely to put that cautious, patient, wary look in Mac's eyes. And she'd seen more than enough of that in the last couple of weeks. So she'd come up with a gaily wrapped package of gourmet jelly beans— five pounds—and since that was one of his secret vices, she figured it would make him smile.

"I'll make sure Mr. Fortune gets the dinner," Ellen promised her.

"Thanks a bunch..." Kelly had just turned around to leave when Mac's office door opened.

A blond beanpole in a suit backed out, saying, "Yes, Mr. Fortune, I'll have it for you by tomorrow."

Following him, one of the chemists in a lab coat hovered another second in the doorway before saying, "Okay, Mr. Fortune. No sweat."

And following him, a chirpy young woman in a navy pin-striped suit and flustered eyes jogged from the office after a fervent, "Right, Mr. Fortune. You're absolutely right."

That seemed to be the end of the "Mr. Fortune" kow-towing, because no further bodies emerged from the inner office after that. Kelly grabbed the satchel and peeked through the open door to see if he were really free. And he was—the office was empty except for her husband, standing with his back to her as he reached for his suit jacket.

"Mac?"

He pivoted around with a startled smile. "What a surprise, Tiny. I was just grabbing my coat to head out for our class."

"I was so sure you couldn't make it that I stopped by to bring you dinner."

"Well, it took moving some heaven and earth. I was positive I'd be late at best, but you know I promised I wouldn't miss any of your classes."

She should have known telling him it was "okay" wouldn't make a difference. Mac never made a promise he didn't keep, and oh, God. Most of the time she was just fine with the relationship they'd settled into. He was patient with her hormonal moods; she was patient with his overprotectiveness. She got a hug before he left for work; they chronically argued about her pink couch; he invariably suggested a short walk after dinner, no matter what the weather—they'd both settled into the routine of living together with more humor and compatibility than she'd ever expected. Mac just didn't want her to be a real wife.

She'd accepted that. She'd accepted that the baby had put their chosen lives on hold for a hiatus of time, and for as long as they were together, she just wanted to be good for Mac. Forget love. In front of her eyes, she could see he was loosening up, laughing more, balancing his responsibilities with more relaxing time. He was still way too hard on himself, but Kelly didn't expect to erode Gibraltar overnight. As long as she was good for him, she told herself it was enough.

Only there were times, like now, when she'd get hit with a wave of love so huge and fragile that her heart ached. He pulled on his navy suit jacket, looking so handsome and self-assured. His white shirt showed off his ruddy skin, made his green eyes so startling and striking. "What's wrong?" he said, when he realized she was staring at him. "Don't tell me I have mustard on my chin from lunch?"

Swiftly she hustled over to straighten his tie. "No mustard. But I was listening to the parade of people kowtowing to you—"

His mouth was already curled in a crooked grin. "Yeah?"

"—And thinking that you sure have them fooled that you're the big cheese. I'm the one who knows you can't even knot your own tie."

"To think I had to get married to get insulted every day." He bent over to smack her nose—as a kiss it could have won land speed records. But it still sizzled her toes. Mac had taken a lot of training to instill the idea that he could volunteer an affectionate gesture. Of course, then he grabbed her arm in a more businesslike fashion. "We're going to be late if we don't hustle. I assume Benz is downstairs?"

"No, I drove myself…" She waited until they were out of the office and he'd say goodbye to Ellen before continuing. "Don't give me that look, Mac. Benz had the sniffles. It was just dumb to drag him out on a cold night when it was just as easy to drive myself."

"You know I'm going to worry about your driving alone until after the baby's born."

In moments, they were winging out of the elevator and through the lobby. She tried to cut off his protective lecture before it started. "Come on, Mac. It's no big deal. I couldn't possibly feel safer. At home, there's the tall gates, the security system, the buzzers and pagers, Benz and Martha. And when I drove in, I had George walk me in from the parking lot."

When Mac pushed open the lobby door for her, she stepped through—and almost bumped into a tall, heavy-set man in a dark wool coat. It was nothing. The man was simply walking fast, not looking where he was going no different than she was. But the sudden gust of frigid night air wasn't the only reason she shivered.

Mac hooked an arm over her shoulder. "That's why." His voice was suddenly rougher than gravel.

"That's why what?"

"That's why I want Benz driving you. You haven't forgotten being attacked, and I'm not about to. If Benz is sick, all you have to do is call me or one of the Fortune drivers to have a car sent."

"Mac, nothing's happened since that one time. I admit it was an awful experience. And I admit sometimes strangers still give me an attack of the willies. But I *am* careful, and I don't want to turn into some paranoid nitwit who sees shadows in every corner. And the more time passes, the more I think the guy who attacked me was just your average run-of-the-mill mugger, not a kidnapper."

"So do I. If someone had been targeting you, something else would have happened by now. Nothing has. And nothing is going to," Mac said firmly, as he handed her into the passenger side of his car. Once he climbed in and started the engine, he continued, "Look, Kel, I know you think I'm overprotective. And you're probably right. But I'm still asking you to cater to me about not driving places alone—at least until after the baby is born."

Well, for Pete's sake. He made it sound like a favor. And Mac knew perfectly well she wouldn't turn him down on something like that. "Have I told you recently that you're a pain in the keister to argue with?"

"Not since this morning," he said dryly. "On the other hand, if you let me win this argument, I'll agree to get rid of the pink couch."

"Yeah? You've said that three times. And I won all three times—but the couch is still there, looking like a pitiful eyesore compared to everything else in the house."

"I like your couch."

"You do not. You're just being nice." And the damn man was always distracting her when he wanted the subject changed. "Look, I heard you on the driving alone. And I'll agree to do it your way, but I want you to quit worrying about it, Mac. No one could have done more to protect me and the baby. Enough's enough. Put it off your mind.''

It wasn't off his mind, Kelly knew. The size of Mac's conscience was bigger than the sky, and his sense of honor was even worse. He shouldn't be feeling responsible for things that weren't his fault or responsibility, but those were touchy waters for a not-quite-wife to bring up with him. By then, the point was moot anyway. They'd reached the clinic and their minds were on the childbirth class.

As they walked in with the others, Kelly noted that the other women all looked a couple of weeks fatter and were moving sludge-slower than last week. Her feminine ego always rose several notches around the other moms. She wasn't the only one doing the duck-walk or who had a hard time getting up and down from the floor mats. Mac eased down next to her. "We should have brought popcorn. We're doing the movie about labor tonight, right?"

"Yeah. Which is partly why I really wouldn't have minded if you missed this one. Mrs. Riley warned us several times that it wasn't the sanitized-for-TV version."

"Pretty graphic, huh? You afraid I'm gonna faint on you?"

"Now, I know you're joking, but she said she lost two husbands in the last class..." Kelly stopped talking when the lights dimmed and the movie started.

She scooched back a little, giving her a better vantage point to keep half an eye on Mac. Men being men, they always claimed to be tough, but sometimes the biggest ones couldn't stand the sight of blood. She didn't figure she needed to pay that close attention to the movie, anyway. Even if she hadn't seen a birth on TV years ago, every mom she knew had filled her in on the birth process. Guys just didn't talk the way women did. She couldn't imagine any educational surprises in the movie.

There were no surprises. But ten minutes into the flick,

her stomach started clenching and her throat went dry. Then came the nausea. Maybe she knew all this stuff. But it was an amazingly different thing, watching the labor process, knowing she was eight months along and this exact thing was going to happen to her in a matter of weeks.

After the class was over, as soon as they got into the car, Mac opened the glove compartment and pulled out a container of saltines. "Maybe it'll help the queasiness," he said gently.

"I'm not going to throw up again," she muttered, but she munched. Several. "I just changed my mind about this whole thing. For the most part I've loved being pregnant. Except for crying at the drop of a hat like a ditsy wuss. And except for needing a bathroom every twenty minutes. But I can live with all that stuff. Indefinitely. I think I'll just grow the baby for another nine months. We don't have to hurry into this labor part of things. Either that or I want to change doctors."

"I thought you loved Dr. Lynn."

"Well, I do. But I already asked her about morphine. She said no."

"Funny, but I could have sworn the last time we left the doctor's office you said specifically that you didn't want any drugs if at all possible."

"That was before I saw the movie. A woman can always change her mind." She crunched down on another cracker. Hard.

"I don't suppose seeing that movie may have changed your mind about wanting a labor coach? Back when we first talked about this, I realize you said no. But you know me better now. If you needed help, I hope you'd know I'd be there."

She hesitated. Her first impulse was to reach over and violently hug Mac, but that was a bonkers thing to do when he was driving in the dark on snowy roads. And although he seemed much more accepting of her need to express affection, that didn't mean he necessarily wanted it. Not from her. So she said, "Listen, you. I appreciate your offering. And if I wanted anyone there, it would be you. But somehow I just feel strongly about doing this alone, Mac. Part of it's what I told you before…that I'm a coward. It's the truth. I'm a wuss. But when I've had to cope with something alone, then I do."

It was Mac's turn to hesitate. "This isn't something where I'd want to argue, Tiny. I just want you to do whatever's right for you. But would you think about it? There's still lots of time to change your mind again."

"Okay."

"I'd be there."

"I know you would."

"And a month from now, this'll be over. We'll have our baby. When you start building up fears in your mind, maybe you want to remember that? Labor's just the bridge to get to the other side—the time when you'll be holding the baby in your arms, bringing it home to that new nursery."

She heard the "our baby." And how Mac had somehow picked exactly the right words to reassure her. No hokeyhearty "attagirls" as if her fears of labor were nothing, just reminding her of the bottom line. The baby. The only thing that mattered. But he mattered, too, she thought fiercely. So many times now, Mac had been a stalwart brick for her, and the lack of balance in their relationship troubled her as it had from the beginning.

He'd never leaned on her for anything. Kelly had had no chance to prove that she'd be there for him. And once, just once, she wished for some time, some chance, for her to be his brick.

Two weeks later, Kelly stood in the nursery window. The view outside was downright ridiculous. It was Valentine's

Day, for heaven's sake. Even the Minnesota weather gods should have figured out it was time to ease up on the raw winter business by now, but no. Even this early in the afternoon, the sky was blacker than gloom and snow was still coming down in fistfuls. The idiot blizzard had started two days before and showed no signs of letting up, the wind still balefully howling, the snow still piling into mountainous drifts. There was no getting out, she knew. Benz and Martha had left for Duluth to visit a grandchild three days before and still hadn't been able to make it back. Mac kept trying to plow them out, but temporarily it was a pointless effort. There was nowhere to go. The roads were all closed, the whole city shut down.

Kelly kept thinking that the weather should be worrying her—particularly since she'd wakened that morning with a piercing backache. Yet Mother Nature seemed to have kicked in one of those strange, pregnancy moods. As if she were surrounded by a protective shell, she'd started the day with a feeling of calm serenity, and nothing seemed to dent it.

She'd stolen up to the nursery for just a few minutes alone. Kneading the ache at the small of her back, she turned away from the window and wandered around the room. It was perfect, she thought. The teddy-bear lamp illuminated all the care and love that had gone into creating the baby's haven. The sheets were already tucked on the crib, blankets ready to snuggle a baby. Diapers waited on the dressing table. She touched the big white rocker, then the colorful mobile over the crib. Maybe the carpet was a mistake—the soft sunny yellow would show dirt?—but she loved it; it was so thick and plush it could surely cushion a crawling baby's knees or a rambunctious toddler's fall.

Her fingers stroked a handmade blanket at the corner of the crib. The baby wasn't supposed to be due for two more weeks. And she'd been ready so far ahead that she figured she'd have to wash and clean everything all over again. But at least right now, she couldn't think of another thing that needed doing.

"Kelly?"

At the sound of Mac's voice below, she took a huge, bracing breath. "I'm up here in the nursery," she called out.

As she could have expected, she immediately heard Mac bounding up the stairs. Even if the blizzard hadn't made them housebound, Kelly doubted Mac would have gone to work and left her alone. The last visit to the obstetrician, she figured he was lucky he didn't get examined right along with her, because he was sticking closer than glue.

He showed up in the doorway, his gaze swooping her up in a single gulp. As soon as he caught her smile, saw she was walking around like normal, the tense muscles in his shoulders seemed to ease. "I saw the cookies cooling downstairs," he mentioned.

"Heart-shaped for Valentine's Day. Pretty corny, huh?"

"I thought they looked like a man's answer to midafternoon starvation. But they also looked so fancy I thought I'd better ask before testing them."

"In other words, you already had—?"

"Three. And God, were they good." That confession out of the way, he ambled into the room, touching things like she had. "I don't know how a baby could have a cooler nursery."

"We did good, didn't we?"

"You're the one who gets the credit, Mom. You planned it and did the tough screwdriver work. I just filled in some of the riffraff brawn." Mac hunched down over the toy chest—his favorite thing. The chest was already brimming with soft things, shiny things, sound-making things—every nature of toy designed to delight someone brand-new to life. "You think it was a little too soon to buy the football?"

"Maybe a teensy bit early—particularly if the baby turns out to be an Annie," she said wryly. "I'll let her play football, mind you, but I just have the feeling you're going to have such an overprotective streak with your daughter that you won't let her date until she's forty—much less play football."

"Hey." Mac feigned a wounded look. "Besides, it could be a boy."

"It could. In fact, I was just thinking that right now, this exact moment, is an ideal time to have a final fight on picking out a boy's name." She took another huge, bracing breath. The last pain had darn near sucked all the oxygen from her lungs.

"We're not having another Mackenzie in the family, Tiny. I hate it when a kid gets stuck with a 'junior' tag."

"But if we called him Aaron Mackenzie Fortune, we can kind of snuggle that name in the middle—so I could get my way—and we could call him by his first name so he wouldn't have that junior problem. We'd both win."

"Yeah, but…hell. What's wrong?" When he noticed her expression suddenly change, he dropped the football and surged to his feet.

It took a second before she could come up with a smile. "It's started. I would have told you earlier, but I wasn't sure. This morning I just thought I had a backache, and later I thought I was just getting more of those false-labor twinges. But as of the last hour—"

"Oh, my God. You mean the *baby?* Oh my God—"

"Now there's no hurry. Everyone says first babies take forever. And I'm not happy about the blizzard, but it's not like women haven't been giving birth since the beginning of time. I put a plastic sheet on my bed, got some linens together, but there's really nothing else to do for a long time yet—''

"You've got those skinny hips! There's no way you're having this baby at home! None! Hell—you just wait right here—'' He galloped toward the door, then galloped back. "No, don't wait here. You need to be in bed, not standing. Why in hell are you standing?"

"Mac, it's okay. Everything's going to be okay. Try and calm down." Kelly couldn't think of a time she'd said those words to him. It was always the other way around. Nothing flustered Mac. Nothing panicked him. He was an oak in a crisis. He never lost patience through all her fitful pregnancy moods, never lost his temper even the third time she'd crashed his computer. She'd never even heard him raise his voice—but his voice was cracking like a hoarse frog's now.

"You're not having the baby at home. You're having the baby at the best birthing center in the country, with exactly the obstetrician and pediatrician we lined up, and I don't give a damn about the blizzard. We'll get you there. Don't worry about a thing. Just stay calm. Just stay easy—''

When the next pain knifed through her, she sank into the white rocker, thinking my God, he was a basket case. He was off. Barreling downstairs with the grace of an elephant. The regular phones were out, but not cell service. He called doctors. He called ambulances. He called cops. In between those frantic, hoarse-yelped phone calls he raced back up to see how she was doing.

She was doing fine—except for fearing Mac was going to have a heart attack. Some time past five, her water broke. Thankfully she was in the bathroom, because she'd have had a fit if she'd been in the nursery and ruined the baby's new carpet. Mac was bringing her ice chips from the kitchen and bellowed her name at ear-shattering volumes when he first couldn't locate her.

"I'm in here, Mac, but I just need a minute alone—"

Possibly he didn't hear that word "alone" because the bathroom door was making too much noise crashing against the opposite wall. Either that or the wild-eyed man barging in was way too panicked that she was in trouble to consider riffraff issues like respecting her modesty. For just an instant, Kelly froze...and he did, too.

She'd just tugged off her clothes and was trying to clean up. A warm wet washcloth was the only thing between her and Mac's eyes. A hundred times, she'd fantasized about being bare for Mac, bare with Mac—but in her fantasy scenarios she'd dreamed his seeing her naked for the first time as a lover. Never like this, with bald fluorescent light glaring and her tummy swollen like a mountain and the mess still not cleaned up from the broken water. She froze for that instant in expectation of feeling embarrassed and awkward...yet that awkwardness never had a chance to develop. He clearly saw. He clearly looked. But barely a millisecond passed before he was reaching for a warm thick towel—to warm her, not to cover her—the difference apparent in the kindling possessive intenseness in his gaze. And for the first time in hours, he slowed down long enough to speak quietly.

"I didn't mean to...I was afraid you needed help and you wouldn't tell me, Kel. It's an insane time to tell you that I think you're the most beautiful woman alive. But this isn't just a moment when I'm prepared to be tactful about what comes out of my mouth. I'm a little shook up—"

"I know you are."

"I'll get over it. It's just..." A hand scraped through his hair like a claw. "We had everything set up, every contingency planned for. The best doctors, the best place, the best everything to make sure the birth went as right for you as it possibly could."

"I know."

"And I get sick at the thought of you in pain."

His vulnerable response to her pain touched her heart more than anything else could have, and so did their crazy gin rummy game.

She didn't remember exactly when her labor coach showed up with those silly cards. After helping her clean up, he moved the plastic sheet and all the linens so the baby could be born in his giant bed. But there was a stretch of time when the labor pains slowed down. Contrary to what she'd ever thought, she was okay with the pain—for damn sure, it was worse than anything she'd ever experienced, but the power of natural instincts helped her keep focused. The baby just wanted to be born. Her body and the baby were simply working together. But in that slow-down stretch, she was feeling discouraged, and that was when Mac brought in the deck of cards. She watched him, hand after hand, fear-sweat beading his brow…yet still concentrating hard enough to cheat and make absolutely sure she'd win.

She thought she'd remember that gin rummy game until she was 105. And the look of his room—the king-size four-poster bed, the dark lake blue carpet, the open door to his closet revealing hangers of proper suits. The room was so Mac. A serious mattress, nice furniture, nothing he was depriving himself of—but no luxuries for himself, no extras. Mac's generosity to others had always been a contradiction to how ruthlessly hard he was on himself, and those intimate hours together underscored both her understanding of Mac and why she loved him. There was simply no way he was a man who could survive labor. He couldn't fix it. He couldn't control it. He couldn't *do* anything to make it easy or right for her. He was miserable.

By midnight, so was she. Elated, miserable, exhausted, sweaty, joyous, irritable. The weather changed. The instant the blizzard winds died, Mac had the cell phone dialed for a Med-Vac helicopter, but she knew it wasn't going to get here in time. So did Mac. They were alone. Just the two of them. And though it had to seem unlikely, she wouldn't have wished for it any other way. Images swirled in her mind. The incredible, precious intimacy of the moment when the baby's head crowned. Mac, suddenly turning calm. Mac, his eyes so intense, so loving, so full of wonder and excitement.

Mac, holding their slippery, squalling daughter in his hands. "You look just like your mom, Annie. Beyond beautiful." And the way he looked at her as he secured the baby in her arms. Then, "I love you, Kelly." The words coming out of nowhere. Just simple. Softly spoken. His heart speaking.

They weren't alone for long. Within an hour, she heard the whir of helicopter blades outside as it landed on the ground, coming to pick up the mom and new baby. She argued about going. The baby was clearly fine. She was beyond fine, once the baby was in her arms, and the bond they'd made together this night was so powerful and precious that she just wanted nothing to come between them. But Mac could only take so much stress that night. He wanted them both in a hospital and no way was he budging.

Not then.

Not about that.

Eight

"Okay. You can sit up now, Kelly. And in answer to the question you're dying to ask me...absolutely yes." Dr. Lynn perched on the examining room stool and clicked on her ballpoint to jot notes in Kelly's file—but not before shooting her a grin. Usually Dr. Lynn's sense of humor made her especially easy to talk to, but this time Kelly didn't have a clue what she meant.

"Well, I heard the 'absolutely yes,' but I'm afraid I'm missing the question," Kelly said wryly.

"Yes, you can have sex with your husband again." Dr. Lynn peered at her over slim black spectacles. "It's always the first question women ask me during this six-week post-partum checkup. And I assume you're a little nervous about having sex this first time after the baby."

"Um..." Never having mentioned her private life with Mac—or lack of—Kelly just hadn't expected this subject to come up with the doctor.

"Well, I give the same lecture to every new mom, so you won't have to worry about asking the same embarrassing questions. It's just natural you'll both feel nervous this first time after the birth. He's afraid of hurting you. You're afraid of being hurt. And both of you are probably worried that going through the labor process changed you physically—to be blunt, that you won't fit together the way you used to fit…"

Kelly didn't have to respond. Dr. Lynn was still going on.

"…but I can ease your mind on that, dear. The night you were flown in after the baby was born, I'm well aware you didn't appreciate my messing with you at the time. But you did tear some, and you may not have wanted those stitches then, but believe me, you'll both appreciate them tonight. Just go slow with each other this first time. Be sensitive that both of you are a little nervous and a little overeager. It'll be fine. Any more questions on that?"

"No."

"Well, I couldn't give you a cleaner bill of health. You're looking great. Nursing going okay?"

"Couldn't be better," Kelly said.

"Good. I'm a supporter of nursing, but I also like what you're doing with one bottle at night. It's tough enough for a new mom to get her rest. That helps. And there's always a chance of your getting ill or tied up sometime, so it's just practical good sense for the baby to know what a bottle is."

Twenty minutes later, Kelly left the doctor's office. A tufty breeze sifted through her hair as she walked across the street to Benz's waiting car. The late March afternoon was chipper, but the wind carried the restless, winsome scent of spring, making Kelly think of love songs.

"Things go okay, honey?" Benz asked when she climbed in.

"No problems. She said I was fit as a fiddle." On the drive home, they passed daffodils peeking out of the ground and dogwoods bursting into early blossom. Benz chatted about Annie and she chatted back, but for once, her breathtakingly beautiful and precociously brilliant six-week-old daughter wasn't on her mind.

Sex was.

Truthfully, making love with Mac had been on her mind darn near incessantly. Before the baby was born, he'd wanted them to have a "think" period. She'd thought. Plenty. Particularly after the incredible night of Annie's birth. But it wasn't as if either of them had a choice right after she was physically recovering from the birth—and suddenly that choice was there.

Kelly gnawed on a thumbnail, unsure if she had the courage to seduce Mac...but damned sure, with his sense of honor, that he'd never pressure her by making the first move unless she'd clearly shown him her willingness.

The black lace negligee Aunt Marie gave her just happened to be hanging in the closet. It wouldn't have fit her even two weeks ago—and her tummy still had a pudge to it—but she was pretty sure it would fit her now. Almost everything else did. A few days before, Kate had dragged her unwillingly away from the baby long enough to have a pamper spree at a salon—hair cut and styled, facial, manicure—it seemed frivolous to Kelly, but Kate claimed every new mom needed that treat. For the first time in her life, she had boobs, thanks to nursing the baby. And besides that, she was healthy and safe and joyously happy over Annie. It all added up to her looking as good as she was ever likely to look in this life.

But that didn't mean Mac would go along with the wild seduction plan spinning in her mind.

"Martha'll be happy as a clam, having the baby to herself for two whole hours," Benz said.

"I hope she didn't cry."

"Now you know she's good as gold right after her nap…"

Maybe she'd make a fool of herself. What did she know about seducing anyone? And Mac…she knew he cared, knew he felt the same electric connection when they touched. But chemistry wasn't love, and Kelly was unsure if he would choose to be married to her if his sense of honor hadn't forced that relationship. He'd spoken of love the night the baby was born, but not since. Nor had he brought up sex again, possibly because he'd changed his mind about wanting to sleep with her…and God, she'd die if he rejected her.

She kept chewing on that thumbnail, those fears building in her mind like mountains. But it still seemed to Kelly that it was time to fish or cut bait. For her, the night the baby was born had sealed every possible loving bond she could feel for Mac. She'd never meant to fall so hard, so deeply, but it was Mac's own darn fault that he'd taught her what real love was. His generous heart had irrevocably opened hers. And Kelly didn't want to add to the responsibility he felt for her…but to never take the risk and show him what he meant to her seemed both cowardly and dead wrong.

If he rejected her, then she would just have to face that. But it wouldn't kill Mac to discover that someone loved him. Not for his money or his power or what he could do or any of that darn fool idiot stuff. But for himself. For the incredibly special man he was. And in the last six weeks, he'd been Annie's father in every sense that mattered, her husband and lover in every sense—but one.

And she wanted him desperately in that one sense, too.

"If this weather keeps warming up, I'm thinking the daffodils and tulips are all gonna pop up in the next week or so—"

"I'm going to do it, Benz, and that's that," Kelly said firmly.

"Huh?"

She recovered swiftly. "Daffodils. I was just thinking I was going to plant some daffodils."

"Good idea, good idea…"

Moments later, they reached the tall locked gates, and then they were home. Startling Kelly, a black sports car was parked in front of the door. Although family had been visiting nonstop since the baby was born, no one had just stopped by without calling first. "I don't recognize that car. Do you know who it belongs to?" she asked Benz.

"Nope, never seen it before."

She came in through the garage, and found Martha waiting for her in the kitchen, wringing her hands on a dish towel. "The baby's still napping upstairs. I got the monitor on down here and I'll listen for her. You got company in the library—"

"What's wrong?" In one glance, Kelly could see Martha's pursed expression. Something had to be bothering her.

"I didn't say anything was wrong. The baby's been an angel. And like I said, I won't budge an inch away from the monitor so I'll hear the minute she wakes up. You just go tend to your company."

"Who is it, Martha?"

"Just go see."

Since Martha would never allow a stranger into the house who shouldn't be there, Kelly couldn't fathom why she was making a minimystery out of some company. But it wasn't as if it mattered; she was going to find out the answer in two seconds. Pushing off her coat, she tossed it on a chair, and tugged on the belt of her cherry red sweater dress as she walked into the library…and then stopped dead on the gulp of a breath.

The man standing at the fireplace was nursing a drink,

wearing slouch-gray slacks and a dark turtleneck. At first glance, a stranger could easily take him for Mac. He had the same glossy dark hair, the same height and lean build, the same striking good looks.

But it wasn't the man she'd hoped to make love to tonight in any way.

"Chad." As soon as she said his name, he pivoted around fast enough to make the Scotch splash in his glass.

"Well…if you aren't looking really fine, Kelly. Being a new mom has to agree with you. You're more gorgeous than I even remembered."

The compliment stung instead of pleased—not because Chad didn't sound sincere, but because Kelly remembered with painful clarity how easily she'd been swayed by that charm when she'd first met him. And all he had to do was turn around to remember that boyish smile and stunning looks. It hurt to realize she'd been too immature to look deeper. He was simply nothing like Mac. There was no honesty in those eyes, no steel in those shoulders, no character lines on that smooth, handsome brow.

She'd known he would come home sometime. She'd known. And because facing him again was unavoidable, she'd tried to mentally plan how to best handle it a zillion times in her mind. Yet fear scuttled through her pulse, distracting her ability to think. Why he was here had too much power to affect her and Mac and Annie.

"You obviously know about the baby," she said carefully.

"Yeah…and just for the record, I didn't when I left. I admit the relationship was getting too heavy for me, and I thought it best to cut loose. I can understand your not wanting to see me again, but I'd at least like you to know that I'd have done something to help you with the pregnancy if I'd known about it."

Maybe he would have, but that was water so deep over

the dam since that it didn't make any difference. Her palms dampened with nerves. "Did you see Annie?"

"Yes. Martha was holding her when she answered the door." Chad paused. "She's a beautiful baby. But I only really saw her for a second. Martha took off with her when she started crying—"

It didn't sound as if he'd even tried to hold her. Some of Kelly's anxiety immediately eased. One of the fears tunneling in the back of her mind was that Chad would take one look at his daughter and form an instant powerful bond. Mac had been irrevocably, lovingly, attached to Annie from the first moment. She'd worried any custody demands would kill him as badly as they would her. "Chad—why don't you just tell me why you're here and what you want? Is there a reason you came home? How did you find out about the baby?"

"Sheesh, you didn't used to be so blunt." When he couldn't rouse a smile, Chad plunked his glass on the mantel. "I came home because Mac tracked me down. I've been on Sunrise—it's a little hideaway island in the Pacific, a good place to soak up the sun and do some skin diving. I don't even know how Mac knew where I was, but I got a wire from him. That was the first I knew anything about the baby or you two being married or anything else—"

"Mac tracked you down?" Her voice came out like a cracked whisper, but the news stunned her like a blow. Mac had never mentioned trying to locate his brother. He'd seemed so happy with her, happy with the baby. She'd been so sure they had an honest chance of turning their marriage into a real one if she just took the first risk with intimacy. But she couldn't imagine a reason for Mac to chase down Chad, especially without telling her, unless she'd misread his feelings—about her. Maybe about everything. For the immediate present, though, she had no choice but to table those worries and handle this situation with Chad.

"Yeah. Mac found me. And the truth is...I don't know how I fit in this. But it seems to me it's up to you. The baby's yours. Maybe you never want the kid to know I'm the father. Maybe you do. Maybe you want financial support from me. Hell, Kelly, I don't have a clue how you want to handle this with the family or the baby or anyone else—much less with Mac."

"How about honestly?" she said with a touch of irony.

"Honestly?"

"A weird concept, isn't it?" She sank into a tufted velvet chair and motioned for him to sit as well. "I don't need or want money from you, Chad. Even before we got married, Mac took care of securing Annie's financial future. And as far as your family—they already know you're Annie's blood father, so there's nothing to hide. I don't believe in hiding from the truth anyway, and the way the Fortune family is so visible in the press, I think it would be nuts to try to keep a secret. Either from outsiders or from Annie. Down the pike, she'll know who fathered her. And who her father is. Those two things aren't necessarily the same."

"What's that supposed to mean? That Mac's taken to being a father, and you don't want me in the picture?"

She hesitated, studying his face. "What I want isn't really an issue. We both created a problem here, and I don't think it's a problem that has any easy answers. I hear your offering to take responsibility, Chad, but I'm looking at your face, your posture—I don't need a crystal ball to figure out that you don't want to be a dad. You don't want to be here at all. And in an ideal world, I'd rather Annie never found out that she was conceived before her mom was married. But people talk. She will hear. And I'd never want to risk her finding out such a thing in the wrong way, from strangers. So my feeling is to pick the right time, be honest with her and then help her deal with it at the time."

"So what are you saying?"

"I'm saying that I just can't guess how these cards are going to play out in the future. I know that I'm not going to lie to my daughter. I know that you and I don't belong together, never did, never will. What I don't know is if you may want to develop a relationship with Annie some time down the road. But if you do, I'm asking you to discuss how to handle it with me first. In fact, I'd appreciate a promise from you that you'd talk ahead with me before doing anything that affects Annie's life."

"For God's sake, what do you take me for? Of course you can have that promise." He frowned. "That's really all you want from me?"

Long after she heard the front door close, Kelly sat in the chair, rubbing two fingers on her temples. Chad obviously never expected this encounter to go so easily. She remembered all that blushing euphoria when she'd first met him, how easily she'd been impressed by his charm and devil-may-care ways. There'd never been love. She knew that now, but somehow she expected to feel something for him besides pity and a certain sadness. He wasn't man enough to realize what he had so easily thrown away.

The difference in brothers was night and day. Mac had depth. Character. Heart. Mac had taught her what real love was, by being a man irresistibly worth loving. Yet her head was throbbing, her pulse charging anxiety. Nagging her mind was why Mac had tracked down his brother. Chad had obviously been summoned home. To see her. Was that supposed to mean that he didn't want her in his life anymore? Could she have misread Mac's caring? Could she have built up crazy false hopes that he could love her?

From the distance upstairs, she suddenly heard the baby's thin wail and swiftly surged to her feet. Annie needed her. And until Mac got home, there was simply no way to know what was in his mind—or heart.

Mac walked in through the door around six. The scent of something delicious simmered on the stove and the table was set, but the kitchen was missing its boss. Kel always rushed in to greet him with her hi-how-was-your-day thing. Amazing how easily a man got spoiled, he thought wryly, and within a second of plopping down his briefcase, he could hear why she wasn't there. Annie was crying. Not loud enough to wake the dead—which he knew his darling was capable of—but she was definitely making her temporary unhappiness with the world known. Quickly he shed his jacket and hiked in the direction of the caterwauler.

His two favorite females were pacing a hole in the library carpet, the baby on Kelly's shoulder, being patted and soothed and there-there'd. His responsive smile was automatic, yet almost immediately his internal antenna picked up that something was wrong. Not with the baby. With Kel. She looked good. Beyond good. The dark red sweater dress snuggled her breasts and hips, teasing his eyes and his hormones. The fire spitting in the hearth gave her skin the glow and luster of a pearl and made her hair look like spun gold. But when she pivoted around and saw him, Mac caught the skittery nerves in her expression.

Something had happened that day. He just didn't know what. But first things first—he smiled a hello and then motioned with his fingers to fork over the monster. "How'd the doctor's appointment go?"

"Couldn't be better, I'm fine. But Annie's been crying for almost an hour. I can't figure out why she's unhappy. She nursed like a pig and I just changed her diaper and she doesn't feel hot or anything like that—"

Being an advanced father of six weeks, Mac had already figured out that baby and mom were tuned to the same channel. If Kelly was dancing around in high spirits, the baby would likely be chortling and cooing. And the rare times Annie was upset, nine times out of ten the trick was easing things for Annie's mom. "Now, you know how smart she is. She probably read the dials on the clock and realized we were going to try to do a damn fool thing like sit down together for dinner. How about if you just go put your feet up for a few minutes? Let me take a turn at calming her down."

"Well...okay. I've been in these clothes all day. I really would like a minute or two to change." Kelly handed over Annie and the usual five miles of blankets, and gave the baby one last comforting pat. "Mac?"

"Just go relax. I'll come find you if I can't get her quieted down, I promise—"

"I will. It's not that...I just wanted to tell you—Chad was here this afternoon."

Adrenaline pumped through his veins in a sharp rush. His gaze darted to her face—and yeah, it was obvious now what had unsettled her. But that didn't mean he could read from her expression how she felt about seeing Chad again.

"We'll talk about it later," he told her. Kelly just nodded and left them.

Mom preferred to do her baby-pacing in the library, but he and Annie had worked out their own routine in the Great room where there was more space—around the pink couch, past the fireplace, a circle around the leather chairs and then pivoting around at the desk. Blankets predictably slipped and bunched, and the baby squirmed, still crying hell-bent for leather. From her pitiful wails, you'd think nobody loved her.

God knew, he did. When a lumberjack-size burp erupted from her delicate rosebud mouth, the tears eased and she seemed to settle in his arms, but Mac wasn't holding his breath the peace would last. His angel was almost twelve pounds now. Old enough to have his number. If Annie was happy walking, they walked, no discussion. All he had to do was look at the tiny, precious face with the wispy tufts of blond hair to feel a wave of unconditional love so huge it swept him under. Still, the last several weeks had been the most harrowing in his entire life.

Failure had never been in his vocabulary before. He was the brick in the family, the one who was always good in a crisis—it was the one thing he'd always been sure of about himself. Yet the night Annie was born, it was still killing Mac that he'd let Kelly down. Instead of being strong, he'd floundered. She'd never said anything about his failing her, but every insecurity he'd ever buried had seeped to the surface that night.

His daughter had brought up more. God knew, all he wanted was to do everything right for her. He'd tried to master the fine art of burping. Tried to get over his terror of drowning her every time he gave her a bath. Tried not to tear down the hall in the middle of the night in panic every time she let out a wail. But the thing was, Annie hadn't come with a rule book. She cried, and there he was in terror land again. No one ever told him that fatherhood was this frightening.

No one ever told him about the loving thing, either. Intellectually, of course, he knew that his brother had contributed the paternal genes—but the first time he held Annie, she became his daughter in every way that mattered. She was the daughter of his heart, the same way Kelly had irrevocably become the love of his heart.

And both the females in his life were the reason he'd tracked down Chad and demanded his brother come home. Everything had gone too far. Kelly had opened his world to emotions he didn't know he had; she was warm and giving and holding back from touching her was driving him crazy. It wasn't right, to complicate her life with an emotionally tangling involvement, without her knowing for sure what she felt about his brother.

Mac believed she needed to see Chad. Face-to-face.

Well, now she had.

Only now, it seemed all those earlier failures mounted up in his mind. There was no question that he had to face this problem. If she had feelings for Chad, then she did. He needed to know—*had* to know—yet the risk of failing to do the right thing, say the right thing, could mean his losing Kelly.

For a man who had never backed down from a principle, Mac discovered that all these years he'd really been an accomplished coward. He watched himself evading Kelly with the finesse of an escape artist for the next few hours.

Dinner was easy. The baby dominated dinner because the baby always dominated dinner. After dishes, Jack thankfully called him on a business problem; then his cousin Garrett called about a personal problem. By that time it was his turn for baby care again and he urged Kel to take a long, soaking bath. The minute she came out, he disappeared into his shower.

By ten o'clock, Mac wasn't proud of his cowardice, but he figured it was late enough to safely hole up in his bedroom...until Kelly suddenly showed up in his doorway. She never did that. She'd always treated his bedroom as if it were his private male bastion—except for the night the baby was born—and he was actually in bed, a book propped on his knees, nothing on but pajama bottoms. His near nudity should have guaranteed that she'd hightail it, too.

Not this time. She stood on the threshold with her arms crossing her chest and her chin jutted out like a bulldog's. The white robe she wore normally made him grin. It was his, an old Christmas gift he'd unearthed from the back of his closet weeks ago, when her own robe just couldn't zip any more over her pregnancy tummy. She usually balked if he tried to give her anything, but she'd confiscated the old robe as if it was a prize, even though the thing drooped on her shoulders and wrists and never stayed tied because the fabric was too slippery.

But her tummy wasn't big now, and nothing about her look in his robe aroused even a pinch of humor. When she stepped into the room, the neck gapped enough for him to glimpse a strap of some shiny black fabric. Glossy, like satin. And black, like Kelly had never worn around him. From the distance across the room, her hair looked brushed with silver, her skin flushed with color, and there was the strangest expression in her eyes.

"By any chance are you avoiding me, Mac?" she asked gently.

"Avoiding you? Of course not...it just seems one of those nights when it's been one thing after another—"

"Uh-huh. And now it's late. Awfully late to start talking about anything serious."

"Really late," he concurred, relieved that she realized the time. Neither used to turn off their lamps until midnight, but that was before the baby. Now parenting had turned them both into zombies by ten. He said sympathetically, "You've got to be tired—"

"Beat," she agreed, and then still studying him with that strange, worrisome look in her eyes, she not only came in but perched on the far edge of his king-size bed. She never sat on his bed. Never. And positively never when he was in it. "But somehow I haven't had a chance to tell you about Chad's visit."

"Well, naturally, I want to hear, but if you're tired we can wait until—"

"The details will wait." Her voice was soft. Soft like the surface of steel. "But I need an answer on something, Mac. From what your brother said, you went to considerable effort to track him down and make him come home. I'd like to know why you did that."

"All right. I did it because..." Restlessly Mac washed

a hand over his face. Hell. He'd never been less than honest with her, but he hadn't avoided this all night for nothing. He'd rather risk his life than risk hearing she still felt love for his brother.

When he didn't immediately respond, Kelly blurted out, "Mac, I have to know. Have you had it with my being your wife? You did the right thing. The baby has your name, but that's done now—the baby's born and everything's different. Maybe you want out, and you thought if Chad came home—"

"Holy kamoly. God. No. That's not it at all, Kel." He heard the suppressed hurt in her voice and it damn near crushed him. And it never occurred to him that she'd leap to such a crazy conclusion. "I wanted you to see Chad. Face-to-face. For your sake. Not for mine."

Her forehead pleated in a bewildered frown. "For my sake?"

He scrubbed his face again. Give him a stock market crash anytime. Anything was easier than trying to talk about emotions, especially when this mattered so much. "Look...you were in love with him—"

"It's been a good year since I believed that, but there was definitely a time I thought I was," she agreed carefully.

"And he hurt you with his irresponsible behavior. But that didn't mean all your feelings for him had died. And I didn't know what your feelings were. I didn't see how you could know. Unless you had the chance to see him again."

She hesitated. "You thought I'd be tempted to take off with Chad if I saw him again?"

"No, I never thought you'd just 'take off.' Hell, I know you better than that. But we both knew that my brother would come back home at some point. And it seemed to me that you were stuck in this uncomfortable limbo place until he did. We didn't set up this marriage to close down choices for you, Kelly, but to open up those choices. You and the baby needed to be safe. But there was never any intent to permanently rope you into a relationship you might not be happy with."

"You think I'm unhappy with this marriage of ours?"

He groped for the right words. "I think...that we've gotten closer, and in different ways, than either of us ever dreamed would happen. But it hasn't gone so far that you still couldn't get out if you wanted out—"

Mac started suffering a strange disoriented feeling. Trying to talk about Chad made him feel more tense than a coiled spring. He'd have thought it would be tough for Kelly, too. Instead, for some bewildering reason, she seemed to be relaxing. She stood up, unfolded her arms and started idly walking around as if moving enabled her to think better. Only the robe sash kept loosening, and the gap at her throat kept widening, revealing smooth white skin and a dipping hint of cleavage. The whisper-sound of satin swooshed against bare skin as she walked. And then there was the strange, unsettling way she kept shooting looks at him.

Mac never thought for an instant that Kelly deliberately intended to give those erotic, exotic peeks of skin, but the thing was, he needed to say everything carefully. He needed to do this right. He needed to be able to think. Only his pulse had picked up a galloping rush, and none of that blood flow was going to his brain—or remotely near that part of his anatomy.

She lifted a hand, just making some kind of expressive gesture. But the body motion further loosened the slippery robe sash, and suddenly the fabric parted to reveal a whole, long ribbon of black satin that drew his eye faster than a drink for an alcoholic. "So," she said calmly, "if I wanted out, it would sure complicate everything if we slept together, wouldn't it? Particularly if you thought I could still be harboring ideas about going back to Chad. Is that what you thought, Mac? That I want your brother?''

"I didn't know.''

"You could have asked me.''

"I wasn't sure if you knew what you felt without seeing him again.''

The damn silky sash fell right to the floor. She didn't even seem to notice, much less seem aware of the view she was exposing him to. ''Well, now I've seen him, Mac. So I can answer that question with no problem at all. There have to be a couple of billion men running around this planet. One of them is your brother. But out of every single man in the universe, I can tell you unequivocally exactly who I want.''

She stepped toward him.

Nine

Mac didn't answer her. Mac just laid there in that giant, king-size bed with one knee cocked up under the navy blue comforter as if he were prepared to talk all night.

Well, Kelly thought desperately, it was up to her. Either she risked her heart—or hightailed it back to her nice, safe, separate bedroom and gave up dreaming about making their marriage a real one.

Seducing him earlier had seemed like such a great plan, but now she felt doomed. Always before, she'd been able to count on chemistry. Desire had always sparked between them. All they had to do was touch. But right now all that nice, combustible chemistry seemed to have flown to Poughkeepsie. Her palms were slick, her stomach clenched with anxiety. Chad showing up had goofed up everything. She couldn't imagine Mac being in the mood—not after all this talking about another man.

Yet with those nerve-damp hands, she slowly reached up

and pushed the robe off her shoulders. It sank to the carpet in a little whoosh. Wearing the sexy black nightgown was the height of dumb, when she knew it showed off her still-pudgy stomach. And offering herself to him was probably plumb nuts, when she was almost positive Mac wasn't in the mood. It would be so much easier if she could wait for another time, another chance, any other night but this one.

But all that talking about his brother was precisely the problem she couldn't walk away from. She'd told him before that she was over Chad. More than once. And Mac just couldn't seem to believe her.

Kelly feared that if she ran away now, they might never get past this. So it was now or never that she bared her heart.

"I want you, Mac," she said lowly. "No one else. There's no other man in my life but you. Not in my mind, not in my heart. You're the only man I want, the only man I can imagine ever wanting. And you don't have to feel the same way, but I want you to believe me—"

Her voice hadn't even started cracking before Mac was vaulting out of that bed. His palms framed her face, pushed back her hair. She only caught one glimpse of the hot green fire in his eyes before his mouth covered hers, claimed hers, in a kiss that made her blood spin.

It seemed…she didn't have to worry about all that electricity hiding out in Poughkeepsie.

They'd kissed before. Not like this. Even a casual hug had provoked chemistry between them before. Not like this.

Lips tasted, savored, clung. His hands swept down the satin nightgown, warming the skin beneath, stroking down her spine to her fanny, rubbing her against him. He only wore pajama bottoms. She could feel the heat radiating from his bare chest, his pounding heart against her pounding heart, his arousal pressing hard and hot against her. In the middle of that wet, openmouthed kiss, he lifted her to the bed.

They tumbled onto the comforter together. Bedcovers bunched. Limbs tangled and twined. She'd known…she'd known Mac had a wellspring of love to give. She'd known from how he was with her, who he was, from every kiss they'd ever shared. But she had no idea how controlled Mac had been until he lost it.

She couldn't catch her breath. Didn't want to. One silver-deep kiss fed into another, chained into another like silver pearls of fire strung together, one inseparable from the last. She tasted hunger on Mac's tongue. She tasted longing. She tasted need, an urgent need that echoed in her own thundering heart and rushing pulse.

She'd been in love with him for so long. She'd feared he didn't care, couldn't care. She'd feared he felt nothing for her but responsibility. But this Mac was as vulnerable as she was. His breath roughened. So did hers. When he palmed her through the slippery satin fabric, her hand sought him to rub and tease. When his mouth dipped down, lips pushing aside the lace bodice to tongue her breasts, her fingers clenched and clawed at his back. She wasn't wild, had never been wild. It was him, fueling these feelings, freeing her as if she'd never been free. So much love was roiling inside her that she couldn't remember inhibitions, couldn't remember fearing inadequacy, fearing anything. Not with Mac. She just couldn't possibly fear anything with Mac.

He pushed at her nightgown, his palm skimming and stroking over calf, thigh, bottom as he chased the garment out of his way. She lifted up, so he could tug the nuisance gown over her head, and then it was gone. She shivered suddenly, a whisper of nerves registering that she wanted to be naked with him, naked emotionally, naked physically…but she had a nursing mom's breasts and a new mom's tummy and fresh white stretch marks. Maybe Mac didn't notice. Mac barely had the nightgown hurled over her head before his mouth was latched on hers again, a kiss that started with her lips and mined a treasure path down her throat to her breasts.

Restlessly she shifted, trying to hook a leg around him. Her breasts had been ultrasensitive since the baby was born, too sensitive, yet it was as if Mac knew. His whiskered cheek nuzzled the tender skin, tickling her, arousing a feeling like fever. Her breasts tightened, swelled, ached, and when his tongue stroked the tight rim of her nipple, desire coiled like a velvet hook in the core of her belly. Yet suddenly Mac lifted his head.

"We have to slow this down." He touched her cheek, his voice rusty, his expression a study in harsh control. "I tasted milk. So sweet, so precious to share...but it hit me like a slap, how rough I was being. I was afraid if I touched you again, this is how it'd be. Not something I could stop. Not something I could control—"

"Forget control. I don't want you to stop."

His lips almost curved in a smile. But the intensity of desire was still in his eyes, still fierce, still grave. "You thought I didn't want you, Kel? It was never that. This was always the problem—wanting you too much. And we do have to slow this down, because I'll have to shoot myself if I hurt you."

"You won't hurt me. And I don't care if you do."

A fingertip nudged her chin, as if he were trying to tilt her face to get a clear look in her eyes. "The doctor. When you went this afternoon. Did the doctor say this was oka—?"

"The doctor said I could do anything I want. She said not to waste any more time talking and that it was perfectly okay for you to love me witless. And that's what I want, Mac. You. Right now. Inside me. Right now."

Possibly Mac didn't quite credit that precise interpretation of the doctor's words, because her lover turned churlish on her. Pokey. Dawdling. She pushed at his pajama bottoms until he made them disappear, but when she finally had him naked, he'd shifted so she couldn't touch him where she wanted. He could. As if he sensed where she felt flawed, he rained lavishly soft kisses on her embarrassingly poochy tummy, traced her new stretch marks with his tongue, kissing with tenderness, touching with savoring reverence. As if they had all night, he concentrated doses of softness, then fire, silken caresses and then the sudden nip of teeth. His hand strayed lower until his palm cupped her, a finger dipping inside, testing her readiness with such gentleness that he couldn't conceivably hurt her...yet still he made no move to take her.

This was madness. She tugged his head up to claim a kiss, closing her eyes, pouring emotion into it. The fire in her belly was long past a blaze, frustration coursing through her like a burning ache that wouldn't be appeased. She wrapped a leg around him, feeling the weight and heat of his arousal. Still he kissed. Still he stroked. The frenzy of touching wasn't nearly enough. Rubbing against him wasn't nearly enough. "Mac..."

He reached out blindly, his groping hand nearly knocking over the lamp. The bedside drawer creaked open. He muttered a swear word before his fingers located a condom. She only realized what he was doing through a hazy fog of sensation. "I'm not going to like this and expect you aren't, either. But you just had a baby, and I'm not risking you, Kel."

"I didn't even think of—"

Suddenly his brow pinched in a worried frown. "I don't want you thinking I had protection because I planned this to happen. There was no plan. I just knew how much I wanted you, and I was afraid—"

She kissed him—to ease away whatever fears he'd had. And to push away her own. She knew making love didn't make a marriage. She knew about Mac's ceaseless sense of honor, but not if his feelings had changed about making a real marriage with her. But this night was about the magic they created together. Nothing else mattered. She wanted Mac to feel loved, and she pushed aside everything else in that quest. Maybe earlier she'd feared being an inadequate bumbling seductress, but Mac seemed to be turning her into an earthy, demanding lover with no trouble at all.

All that other heat was just smoke. This was fire. When he swept her beneath him, her arms were already pulling him in, pulling him down, impatient for the feeling of him inside her. Slowly he probed, easing in with exquisite care until he was absolutely sure she could take him, but then that slowness was done. Longing, luscious and liquid, pulsed through her veins at those first strokes of possession. Excitement, heady and wild, charged through her heart on a race toward ecstasy after that. This was right. Nothing in her life had ever been this right. She belonged to him. With him.

He thrust and withdrew, again and again, each time accelerating the rush in her heart, each time giving them both a taste of almost, almost, reaching the peak of completion…until she was arching for him, clinging to him, her breath was as raspy as his, her heart thundering in unison with his.

"I love you, Kelly. Love you…"

She felt his love more than hearing the words, and it tipped her over the edge. She called his name on a sharp cry as pleasure speared all through her, one wondrous spasm cresting into another and another. And when it was over, Mac sank onto the same pillow, as spent as she was, the kiss on her temple the last thing she remembered.

At three o'clock, Mac heard the baby's distant cry. Although Kelly's eyes were still closed, she automatically stirred in his arms. "Shh, no, don't wake up. I'll get the tiger," he whispered. She was snuggling so tightly around him that it took a minute to ease away from her and climb out of bed, but she promptly drifted off again.

He padded down the dark hall into Annie's room. A night-light illuminated his daughter's cherubic face and the rosebud mouth already open to let out another plaintive wail. He halfway expected hunger was the problem, even though she'd been skipping the middle of the night bottle for a week now, but it wasn't that. Instead she'd flipped over on her back—her newest acrobatic move—and was whimpering frustration at being unable to turn herself back over. He gently eased her onto her tummy, but after a couple of soothing pats, she drifted back to sleep, too.

It seemed everyone was snoozing great this night but him. Trying to be as soundless as a cat, he walked back into the bedroom. Moonlight shone from the French doors on the curve of Kel's cheek, her tousled pale hair. She'd scooched over to his warm spot and stolen all the covers, making him smile, but recalling their lovemaking put a worry beat in his pulse.

Stark naked, he opened the French doors and stepped out. The woods were silent, breathless, the green-young scent in the air promising spring, but the night was still bite-cold, the decking like ice beneath his bare feet. The sudden bracing cold suited his restless mood. From the shadowed woods he heard the lonely, mournful cry of a hoot owl, calling for his mate. There so obviously was no mate. Night after night, the owl kept up with that incessant hooting. Mac could never figure out why the damn owl couldn't accept his loneliness, move on, take care of business, do whatever owls did with their lives.

But after tonight, Mac felt on an empathetic wavelength.

Being alone wasn't the same as loneliness. Once a guy discovered what having a mate really meant, nothing was right without her.

"Mac? What's wrong?"

Hearing Kelly's sleepy voice, he immediately stepped back in and latched the door. "Nothing. Everything's fine. I didn't mean to wake you—"

"You didn't...I was sort of half awake from the minute I heard Annie cry. She's okay?"

"She was fine. Just practicing her acrobatic flip-over thing..." He slid in beside her, making her yelp in startled humor.

"You horrible man! You're freezing! And those hands are like icebergs!" He'd have removed his offending iceberg body parts, but she'd already grabbed his hands and was kneading them warm with her own. And then she snuggled full-length against him to warm the rest of his cold body, too. "You couldn't sleep?"

"I've always been more of a catnapper than a solid sleeper."

"Like your daughter." When she finally warmed him up to her satisfaction, she took over his shoulder as if it were her personal pillow. "If I haven't told you before...you're an incredibly wonderful dad, Mac."

Her whispered praise made him feel warmer yet. He'd told himself a dozen times that he was too old to need approval, even from Kelly. But it deeply mattered to him, that Kel not only completely trusted him with the baby, but had never referred to Annie as anything but his daughter. The way she snuggled a leg between his, though, there wasn't a single fatherly thought in his head. "You're a natural mom."

"I was always crazy about kids. You going to tell me what's troubling you?"

"Nothing. Really."

"Uh-huh. I'm not buying that Brooklyn Bridge. If you were standing outside in the pitch cold at three in the morning, something was on your mind." She hesitated, her voice suddenly turning silky-light as if just making idle chitchat. "Are you regretting what we did?"

"No." His lips pressed to her temple—a damn dumb thing to do when her supple warm body was already reigniting desire. But he couldn't have her doubting that even for an instant. "I'll never regret making love with you."

The way her soft eyes turned luminous, she'd needed to hear him say that. Like a stubborn hound, though, she wasn't finished probing. "Then it was something else bothering you. Mac...you can't possibly believe I still have feelings for your brother?"

"No." His voice came out quiet, firm. She'd left him no doubt whatsoever whom she loved. Or that she felt love.

She hesitated again, as if determined to uncover whatever had troubled him. "There's only one other thing I'd like to bring up about Chad. It occurred to me tonight, that maybe you'd have believed me before—if I'd just been more clear, more frank. But it was hard to be frank, when I didn't—and don't—want to put him down to you. Maybe you two aren't close, but there's a loyalty of blood there. I don't want you shutting a door because of me."

"He hurt you." Instinctively his fingers sifted through her hair, a caressing gesture. A protective one.

"Maybe, but that's past tense. I don't feel hurt now. I do feel some lingering shame—that I was so foolish and naïve—but that blame's on me, not on your brother. But I *would* feel hurt, Mac, if I were responsible for causing a rift between you. I know you don't respect your brother's behavior or lifestyle. But he can't ski through life without coming to the bottom of the slope sometime. I think he's lost. As a man. If there ever comes a time he wants to make something of his life, I think you're the only one he even thinks about listening to."

"Tiny...did I ever tell you that I think you're ten feet tall?"

"Huh?"

"You're the last person in the universe I'd expect to give him any sympathy. I won't shoot him. I promise. And I won't forget he's my brother, even if I feel like shooting him. I promise that, too. I'm even glad we got all this sticky air cleared, but can we quit talking about this now?"

Immediately she murmured, "It's ridiculously late. I don't know why you started this discussion, for heaven's sake. You know what a full day you've got tomorrow, and you need your rest. Now just close your eyes and go to sleep."

Damned if she didn't make him grin. She was the one who had started this whole hairy discussion in the middle of the night. She was the one coping with Annie all day and who needed her rest. Sometimes—okay, often—she completely bewildered him with her pure-female thinking.

And then there were other times. Like now. When her pure-femaleness ransacked every sane thought in his head. As if she'd slept with him forever, she naturally snuzzled up tighter against him. He heard her soft sigh. Her warm, bare breasts molded against his chest. Her silky hair tickled his nose; the scent of her skin drifted like an aphrodisiac to his nose, and she bent her leg, edging her upper thigh against his arousal.

He was harder than stone—had been from the minute he climbed back into bed with her. But there was no question about their making love again. It was too soon after the birth; he'd been conscious of her being tender and exquisitely sensitive that first time, and he hadn't been as gentle as he should have been. He'd been petrified of hurting her, but her earthy, passionate responsiveness had gone straight to his head. It was his job to take care of her. His right, as her lover and husband. And knowing now how dangerously she uncorked his self-control, there was no chance—none—of their making love again tonight.

"Mac?" she murmured.

"What?" Hell, he'd been praying she'd fallen back asleep.

"I just want to tell you one more thing, and then I swear I won't say another word. I promise."

"Okay."

"I know this is the nineties. And some of the old traditional values—we just don't feel that way anymore. And I don't, either. But I just wish...that I'd been a virgin for you, Mac."

When she twisted her head so that he could see her eyes in the darkness, Mac mentally swore. He had to kiss her. She wasn't giving him any choice at all.

Her hand climbed up his arm, skimmed over his shoulder and then roped around his head to coax his mouth on hers. Her slim, lithe body arched against his both in vulnerable yearning and invitation.

In his head were a thousand worries that this was wrong. Loving her...he couldn't help that. But loving her made it all the more important that he not fail Kelly, and haunting his heart was a new, painful awareness that he wasn't strong. Not near her. Maybe she was okay with his blundering fears the night Annie was born. Maybe she hadn't guessed how unsure he felt at doing the right things as a father. And maybe they'd even settled the business of Chad.

But whether Kelly really wanted to be married to him was a question of another color. She'd married him because she needed protection. That need was real. No one could be more vulnerable than a pregnant woman, and Kelly had particularly been unschooled in the kinds of problems affected by wealth and influence. Everything about the pregnancy and new baby had put her normal life on hold for a while. But Kelly was healing from the birth. Her choices were going to be very different shortly.

Honor had never been a lip service word to Mac, but the code of how a man lived with himself. He didn't want to pressure her about what she did or didn't want this marriage to be…and their becoming physically involved unquestionably complicated their relationship emotionally. He wanted to do the right thing. Needed to do the right thing. To give her time.

But honor didn't seem worth dried beans. Not when he was holding her, never when he was kissing her. She was the mate that the hoot owl kept crying for. The woman he'd never expected to find. The wonder of his life, the sunshine. And he could no more resist making love with her than he could stop himself from breathing.

Most people daydreamed about money. For the most part Kelly thought of the Fortune money as troublesome—more worry than fun—but the domestic scene, now, that was her daydream. And this morning was just about perfect. Sunlight streaming in. Birds singing. Blueberry pancakes sizzling in the skillet. Annie cooing from her baby seat, next to an adorable man with a hickey on his neck. Mac, asking about her day, with one hand on the baby and the other on the morning paper.

Kelly flipped the pancakes. "Me, I have nothing special on my agenda today. I just plan to loll in lazy decadence. But Annie now…she plans to make cookies this morning, and then do an exercise video, and then take a big noisy bath…and after her nap—if it really does warm up to sixty…I have my doubts the weatherman was telling the truth—she told me she wants to stroll outside and soak up some spring sunshine."

"Sounds exhausting to me. But if Annie's mom isn't too

tired from that day of sloth, maybe Martha and Benz could baby-sit and the grown-ups could slip away and go out to dinner.''

Kelly's head shot up. No sense in taking this domestic bliss business too far. "Out to dinner?"

"You know. It's when there's no dishes to do, no cooking, someone else waits on you. I know it's a wild concept, but—"

"I'm ready. What time?" Mac grinned at her obvious enthusiasm. She was just about to grill him—she wanted the details pinned down in blood—but just then the telephone rang.

She hooked the receiver in the crook of her shoulder as she spatulaed pancakes onto a platter. "Well, hi, Aunt Marie, how nice of you to call…" Twisting the phone cord to reach the table, she kissed the top of Annie's head—who was helping Mac read the morning paper—then Mac's head, then set down the platter. "Why yes, we knew Chad was in town…yes, we've seen him…yes, he saw the baby, uh-huh…uh-huh…well, no, actually…"

A few moments later she hung up the phone and plopped down at the table next to Annie. "Now, about the time for this dinner tonight—"

Mac swallowed a mouthful of pancakes. "Are you getting a lot of those calls from my family?"

She lifted her finger in a "wait" gesture, because the telephone had rung again and she was already charging out of her seat to grab it. This time the call was Renee, and Kelly had barely had a chance to talk with her maid of honor since the wedding. "Hi, you, I…you're kidding! I wondered what happened when you disappeared right after the service, but I'd never have guessed anything like that. I can't believe your dad is serious. Come on, sweetie. No one can make you marry anyone. It's not like this is the Middle Ages. I…yes, Chad is home. You heard too, huh?"

Kelly started piling dishes into the sink, since she was already up. "No, no…really, it's gone just fine…yes…forget Chad, I'd rather talk about your problem with this guy. Okay, but if you need any help, I want you to call us, you hear me…?"

It took another minute before she could hang up, and then Kelly whirled around to tell Mac the story about Renee—he knew her, too, and maybe could offer some advice on the problem Renee was dealing with. But Mac was distinctly tuned to another conversation channel, and right then he obviously didn't want to let the subject drop.

"Kelly, how often are you getting calls about Chad like that?"

"Well, since your brother came home last week…I'd say the phone rings once every couple of hours," she said wryly. "Sooner or later I figure they'll quit, but it seems right now their curiosity is at an all-time high. And I hate to admit this, but I'm afraid I'm a big disappointment to your family. They keep hoping for some nice, juicy dirt and scandal, and I think they're disgusted with me. I'm not coming through."

"Annie, tell your mom that she's supposed to tell me what people are giving her a hard time. What good's a husband if he can't slay some dragons for you now and then?"

"Annie, tell him that husbands are good for going out to dinner."

"Yeah, Tiny, well, I'm just waiting for you to name the place. What's your poison? Lobster, steak? You want soft lights and quiet, or some live music and a little razzle-dazzle—?" When the phone jangled again, Mac wagged a finger at her. "I'll get it this time."

Kelly watched him bark a "hello" into the phone, obviously prepared to tear a strip off the hide of any further nosy relatives…and then noted with amusement when his expression changed. Dryly he handed her the phone. "It's Kate. And she wants you." To Annie, he murmured, "Cripes, there went my credibility as a dragon slayer. And nobody wants me anymore. They all want your mom."

She was still chuckling as she fended the call from Mac's great-aunt. This one wasn't quite so intrusive and only lasted a few minutes—just long enough for her pancakes to get cold, although she dove right back in again.

"I'd hate to kill Kate," Mac admitted. "She's been damn good to me, but if she's part of this gossip brigade—"

"No, no. She just asked me for lunch next week. At Fortune's. She wants me to bring the baby in to show her off. And rather than put Annie through a restaurant setup, she's going to order lunch in her office."

"Knowing Kate, she's envisioning starting another generation of Fortunes early. Although maybe she suggested that lunch for another reason—like about you." His gaze suddenly rested for a long moment on her face. He could still make her flush, even after a week of long, wonderful nights together. By day she might run around smelling of baby powder, wearing jeans and no makeup, but he made her feel like an entirely different woman when the lights went off. "Kelly, are you getting tired of staying home? You always seemed to love working for Kate. And God knows, she sang your praises upstairs and down about how terrific you were."

"Actually she already asked me to do a gala thing—a press party for a new line of skincare. But that's in July. I'm thinking about it. To be honest, I really don't want to be away from Annie. I don't want to miss any of these moments of her first months and first years if I don't have to. But if Kate just comes up with just an occasional project she wants me to handle...I don't know, Mac. What do you think? Would you have a problem with my working?"

"I don't have a problem as long as you're happy. But Jack's been giving me advice. He says nonstop baby care is too exhausting and you might need a break from it. Of course Jack's divorced, so his advice about women and new moms might not be the best in town."

She chuckled. "I don't need a break. But maybe I will some months down the road. Right now there's so much I want to do. I haven't even been back to my old apartment to get my summer clothes, or to do anything about closing the place up."

"No hurry. The rent's paid up. Nothing needs to be done."

Kelly felt a restless qualm. The new intimacy between them had been more than she ever dreamed of and then some. But while she was sleeping in Mac's bed, her clothes still hung in the closet in her old bedroom. And though she'd mentioned a willingness to get rid of her old apartment, this was the second time Mac assured her that the lease was paid, as if it were okay with him if she kept the place. Both issues made her worry that Mac still didn't see their marriage as a real one—or that he didn't want the relationship to be permanent. "If Annie and I get some free time today, we just might throw out that pink couch."

"Annie, tell your mother I have another idea. She can decorate the rest of the room in pink, and then the couch will fit in, and then she'll quit yanking my chain about it…are you going to go to that lunch with Kate?"

"Yes. It sounds like fun." And she had to grin about his bulldog attitude on the damn couch. It was the only long-running argument they had. Both seemed to enjoy the teasing bickering too much to solve the silly problem. She also felt reassured—at least for now, he was surely not tired of her if he was still being stubborn about keeping the couch.

"I'll have Benz drive you. What day is this lunch?"

"Tuesday. But I don't want Benz stuck sitting in a car for two hours. It's just silly. I can drive myself."

Mac glanced at his watch, wiped his mouth with a napkin and dropped a kiss on his daughter's brow as he stood up. Kelly stood, too, automatically walking him to the door and reaching out to fix his tie. Like an old married couple, she thought. Or almost.

"Benz loves driving you," Mac said. "It's good for him, besides. He's getting older and doesn't want to admit it. He starts doing physical chores around here and won't say quit. If he's driving you somewhere, it's an easy break for him—"

"You're still trying to wrap me in cotton wool, husband. But I'm not waddling pregnant anymore. And I'm not as naïve as I used to be about safety. And we were just talking about my doing an occasional work project for Kate—"

"But that's months away. And she's as obsessive-compulsive about safety as I am."

She nodded. After fixing his tie knot, she picked a non-existent fleck of lint from his navy suit jacket, then followed through with the rest of their new morning ritual by roping her arms around his neck. His head was already cocked, mouth slanted to meet hers, take hers. She mined his lips for a treasuring taste of pancakes and coffee and him. It was magic. Every time. Tension electrified his body, then hers. Need rose up like a volcano of vital, hot, shimmering desire. His hands swept down her spine, cupping her bottom, body parts he surely knew he owned now, yet still it was new. This feeling of belonging to him. This feeling of wanting so sharp it took away her breath—and his, too. When Mac lifted his head, those cool gray-green eyes of his weren't cool anymore.

"Were we arguing?" he murmured.

"Yes."

"Did I win this one or did you?"

"Me."

"You always say that. You're turning into a bossy, manipulative woman, Tiny. You know damn well kissing you turns my mind to mush."

"Oh, well," she murmured, and made him chuckle. But only for a second.

His forehead puckered in a serious frown. "Maybe I am a little obsessive-compulsive about the driving. But I just can't seem to entirely forget that guy who attacked you."

"Neither can I," she admitted honestly. "But that's exactly why I've had enough of this coddling. It's been months. I need to get over it. Being careful is one thing, but building up fears that there could be danger in every shadow is goofy. I need to get out and do some things alone."

"All right. I hear you. I just...I *need* to know you're safe, Kel."

She knew he worried about it. Too much. But once he left and she turned to the breakfast dishes, a sudden lump welled in her throat. The irony hit her—between security systems and protection and pagers, she really couldn't possibly feel more physically safe. The only place in her life she felt unsafe was with Mac.

Increasingly she felt shaky, as if her heart were on shifting sands with nothing solid in sight. Sex had changed everything. She'd made love with him freely, given herself freely, never to tie Mac to her. That was the story she'd sold herself, but it was a lie. She'd hoped it would matter. She'd hoped that chemistry would add up on top of everything else—the baby, the baby's birth, the honest relationship they'd both worked hard to build together.

She'd always known that she was nothing like the tall, sophisticated women he'd taken out who were savvy in the business world. But she wanted to believe that she was good for him. He laughed so much more. He'd loosened up, was starting to share problems and feelings, and she really had no doubt the chemistry was powerful for both of them. But none of that was enough to snare his desire for a real marriage. Not unless he felt the right kind of love.

He'd married her from a sense of responsibility. She knew that. But possibly that dreadful character trait was infectious, because now she felt responsible—and honor bound—to not force a tie if it didn't make him happy. Their time together was good. But Kelly sensed that something needed to happen, and soon, because neither would be content in this precarious place of an "almost marriage" for much longer.

Ten

Kelly slipped into red high heels and stood up with a wince. Flats would be more comfortable. Wearing heels for a dinner out with Mac was fun, but just going to lunch with Kate didn't seem worth the discomfort. On the other hand, she'd looked like an unkempt pregnant whale the last time she'd walked into the Fortune Company lobby. And her navy dress with the red piping really spiffed up with the red heels.

She glanced at her daughter, who was vigorously waving her fists from the middle of the bed. "So what do you think of the shoes, Annie? Should we go for sensible or vote for vanity?"

Annie, being born female, seemed to express more enthusiasm for the vanity vote. Kelly concurred, figuring the two of them would be sitting most of the time anyway. Still wearing the heels, she was just plugging ruby studs into her ears when the telephone jingled.

"Mollie!" Kelly sank on the bed with one hand idly playing with the baby. "It's about time we caught up. I tried to reach you a couple of days ago, but all I got was your answering machine. I was worried...the last time we talked, you said you were trying to work out a problem—"

"I got a couple of new wedding jobs to bid on, so I've just been running nonstop. But I started worrying how you were doing, too. You too busy to talk?"

"I'm going to lunch with Kate—taking Annie—but I don't need to leave for another few minutes. You okay with that problem you were dealing with?" Kelly asked.

"Not okay. But I know what I want to do. It's just taking some time to work up to it. You try and bury a problem, it just festers, you know? And like my mom always used to say, if something really matters to you, you can't win anything sitting on the sidelines. You have to go for the gusto...I'll tell you more about that later. Right now—how's our princess?"

"The princess is dressed befitting royalty. A pink sleeper with white satin bows, her hair brushed into a curl, rattle matching her pink outfit...of course, the drool kind of spoils the effect, but what can you do? And I'm taking three other outfits to this lunch because I know how fast she goes through them. But temporarily, she's blowing bubbles and looking incredibly elegant."

Mollie laughed. "I love it when you talk about her. You're really loving being a mom, Kel."

"Every minute. Even the no-sleep and the colicky minutes." For just an instant Kelly squeezed her eyes closed. "I just wish my mom were here to see her."

"Yeah, I miss my mom, too. All the time. We fought too much about dumb things, like curfews and makeup and boys. But it didn't matter. There were still things I could talk out with my mom differently than with anyone else."

"I know. It was the same with my mother...." Kelly

sighed. "It was the first thing I thought when I found out I was pregnant. That my mom would be so disappointed in me. It was the one thing she never let up on—watch out for guys with charm...don't make the mistake she made..."

"Your mom would have understood a Chad, Kel. She fell for one herself. And all that's behind you now. Speaking of which—how's marriage going?"

"Mac is spoiling me rotten. Took me out to dinner twice this last week. Came home with a bouquet of camellias yesterday, then out of nowhere put a box on my pillow—ruby earrings, I'm wearing them. In fact, picked a whole outfit to go with them. But all the things he's doing are kind of scary—"

"Scary?"

"I don't know why he's doing all this stuff."

"God, you're such a dimwit. For the first time in your life, you're being spoiled and you have to look for reasons?"

"But I haven't done anything—"

"How about that the man's in love with you?"

When Kelly hung up the phone, it was almost eleven-thirty. Time to scoop the baby up and head for Fortune's if they were going to make their lunch date on time. But the whole conversation with Mol had invoked her feelings about Mac, and just for a few seconds, her mind spun back to the evening before.

Annie had been fractious all day, and after dinner, Mac had taken charge of the baby and she'd gone upstairs to soak in a hot, jasmine-scented tub. It seemed only minutes had passed before the door suddenly opened, and steam swirled around in fragrant clouds from the abrupt gush of cool hall air.

But then he'd closed the door. And turned out the light. And slipped naked with her into the tub. She could have guessed Annie would settle down and go to sleep like an angel for her dad. But settling down very clearly wasn't on Mac's mind, nor was behaving like an angel.

Images swam in her mind. Textures, scents, sounds. The smell of jasmine in the darkness. His slick wet body teasing her slick wet body, water sloshing everywhere, his lusty laughter. He seemed to have a hundred hands, all of them slippery and wet, all of them invoking wicked sensations and shameless fantasies. She'd thought of the formidably formal Mac he used to be—the Mr. Fortune he still was for the world—but the man in the tub with her was an amoral, unprincipled pirate, determined to steal her virtue and seduce her without mercy. Passion spiraled between them until he fit her on top of him, and after all these nights, she could have sworn she didn't have an inhibition left. But she remembered turning liquid for Mac, boneless for Mac, a part of him like she hadn't known a woman could be part of a man.

Her eyes squeezed closed. She'd woken up that morning feeling fragile and shivery and giddy-high from the inside out. Mac had used words of love before—in passion, and the night the baby was born. But those times had been so emotionally charged that she'd been wary of believing he meant it. Last night had mightily reassured her fears. She knew Mac still felt a powerful feeling of responsibility for her, but he'd shown her love in so many ways. They *had* a real marriage. It was surely just a matter of time before he realized it, too.

Annie suddenly let out a squall. Startled, Kelly turned around and then swiftly scooped her daughter into her arms. "Okay, lovebug, I'm impatient to hit the road, too. You didn't think I'd forgotten about lunch, did you? As if I'd miss an opportunity to show you off."

Outside, it was a joyful April day, with a balmy sun and a dancing, susurrous breeze. Mac had left her the black

Mercedes for this excursion—which was a zillion times fancier than the economy compacts she used to drive, so it took a moment to become familiar with all the dials, get Annie strapped in the car seat and all the baby gear stowed away. And then they were off, with Annie chortling next to her, seeming delighted with their outing. Daffodils, tulips, dogwood and yellow forsythia were all bursting in bloom, and driving through the woods, all the trees were leafing out, dressed in all their starchy new greens, creating sun-dappled shadows and the sweet-young smells of everything coming to life. Of course, then she hit the outskirts of Minneapolis and city traffic.

"Now, just be good for ten minutes for me, Annie. We'll be there in two shakes...."

The car was an angel on the road, and it wasn't like trying to cope with rush hour besides. The roads were simply crowded around noon. Moments later, she pulled into the lot next to Fortune's, and waved to George, the guard. He was on the phone, but waved back. It was silly to feel reassured that he was there, when she'd told Mac—how many times?—that both of them needed to completely forget about that past assault. Anxiety didn't belong on a gorgeous spring day like this, but just then, she didn't mind agreeing with Mac about letting George walk her and the baby into the building. She hated bothering George, but Mac was so darn hyper about safety that she'd made the concession.

Finding a parking place was her first problem, though. Half the city seemed out and about, taking advantage of the spring day, shoppers and business people and everyone else trying to nail down a parking place during the lunch hour. She finally found a spot near the east entrance.

"There now, sweetie pie. Time to get organized..." First, she reached over and unstrapped Annie from the car seat. Then scooping up her purse, she pushed at the rearview mirror to tilt it, ran a fast brush through her hair and applied some fresh lipstick, then unlocked the doors and swiveled her legs out. The diaper bag was stashed in the back seat. She fetched that, then propped both her purse and bag on the hood. Then...

Then chaos.

God. It just couldn't happen. Couldn't be happening. There were people everywhere. There was George, right at the north entrance in his little guard shack. And she was standing at the driver's side of the car, not moving slowly, not doing anything careless, just seconds away from crossing in front of the car hood to get to Annie's door. In seconds she'd have had the baby in her arms. In seconds.

But the man...he was just suddenly *there,* yanking open the passenger door and grabbing Annie. Blondish hair. Gaunt cheeks. He was youngish, like in his twenties, wearing khakis no different than the whole world wore and an innocuous sweatshirt—the flash of recognition came from realizing that she'd already noticed him walking in the parking lot, but there was just nothing to make her think he wasn't striding purposefully to reach his car like everyone else.

"Stop! Don't you *touch* her, you—" She crashed her hip into the car hood, trying to fly to the baby's side, no air getting to her lungs, nothing in her heart or head but panic—and getting to Annie.

But it was too late. She shrieked at the top of her lungs for help, but the man already had her—she saw the baby's head jerk back the way he snatched her, the pink blanket flapping as he wheeled around and started running. For a split second she froze in indecision, not knowing whether to chase him or get help. If summoning a cop was the best choice, her mother's heart simply couldn't make it. She couldn't possibly let him disappear from sight with her baby—nothing was more terrifying than that—so she took off after him, her heart pounding like a racehorse, her hip screaming where it had bumped metal. That split second hesitation had given him a lead, but he wasn't that far away. She'd catch him.

She had to catch him.

He whipped across the street against a red light, dodging cars, making brakes screech and horns blare. She whipped after him, screaming for help, screaming for her daughter. A red van almost hit her; she crashed into an older woman shopper laden with packages. Tears blinded her eyes, frantic, infuriating tears that affected how clearly she could see, and he was gaining yards on her. Her three-inch heels were slowing her down; she kicked them off and kept chasing him, ignoring the bite and scrapes of concrete on her stocking feet.

Strangers stopped, obviously confused by the reason for a woman running hell-bent for leather down the city streets—maybe they would have helped, but their stopping only impeded her trying to duck and dodge around them. The man turned a corner, ran down an alley between tall concrete buildings, then clambered around another corner. When she caught up, her lungs were heaving and the stitch in her right side cut like a knife…but suddenly he was gone.

No sign of him. Nothing. There were buildings everywhere. Street traffic. A taxi zooming past, pedestrians staring at her—but no blond man with a pink blanket flapping behind him. Dozens of doors lined the street, doors to businesses and stores and everything else—he had to have gone in one of them, but which? A wrong guess could mean the difference in her baby's life. A wrong guess could mean…

Fear clenched her heart in a tight fist of agony. A stranger had Annie. A kidnapper. Her worst fear, Mac's worst fear…and nothing in life could have given her a more unbearable punch in the soul.

She had to find their baby.

She had to.

Mac had a meeting with four men in the office when his secretary poked her head in. "I need you, Mr. Fortune."

Mac promptly excused himself and followed her into the outer office. "What's wrong?"

"I don't know." He knew there was trouble—she'd never have interrupted him otherwise. But in the ten years they'd worked together, he'd never heard Ellen's voice quiver or seen her hands shaky. "Something is. George is beside himself...I've got him on line one—"

"George?" He was already reaching for the phone

"George, the security guard in the parking lot..."

The instant she identified which George she meant, Mac's heart started to slam. And then he heard the guard's croaking voice. "Somebody got your baby, Mr. Fortune. I got a look at him. I got the cops called right away. I saw it all. I was right here when Mrs. Fortune drove in, watching for her so I could walk her in, you know, like we set up. Only I was on the phone, and she hadn't parked yet so I'd know where she'd be, because I would have headed right for her, only it all happened so fast—"

"George—" The guard was talking so fast he was stuttering.

"Your cousin was right here in the lot, going to lunch, saw it, too, went after him, too...but Mrs. Fortune, she was really running, and the other Mr. Fortune, he stopped like I did, thinking to call the cops, and she was out of sight so fast. And I'm so sorry I'm sick. I swear I was watching for her, and I wasn't that far away, and there were people all over the place, company people. Nobody'd be so crazy to kidnap a baby in broad daylight in front of everyone like that and I just—"

"George. Stop. Take a breath. *Where* is my wife?"

"I don't know, sir. She's gone. She just tore after him…ain't nobody was gonna stop her. I yelled out, so did Sam Johnson, you know the chemist who works up on three, but I'm telling you, nobody could have made her stop. I— Oh, I see the cops pulling in right now—"

"Tell the police everything you know. Don't wait. Don't wait for anything. Get them going after her. And I'll be right there."

In every life crisis Mac had been through, he'd turned cool and controlled. Battering down the hall, down the elevator, blasting through the side door to the parking lot, he couldn't get to that steel layer of cool. It seemed as if something hot and acid was pumping through his lungs. He could breathe it. Guilt. Blame. Scissoring up to the surface like a volcanic fissure that was cracking at the seams. Cracking him. At his seams.

He couldn't survive if something happened to Kelly and the baby. Not a chance. Not a prayer. He couldn't lose her. He couldn't lose either of them.

A thousand pictures replayed in his mind in those seconds he was charging toward the cop cars and uniforms and people milling around and George. Their wedding night, when she'd offered him a chaste kiss that rocked his world. Her blubbering when she couldn't tie her shoe laces. The radiance in her face when she'd cradled the newborn Annie in her arms. Her politely explaining the need for her hugs, her yelling, "Mac, you're home!" as she hurled around a corner, her singing off-key when she made cookies. Her buttery-soft laughter in the darkness, making love with her in the tub, making her come alive, watching his love turn sultry and sassy and sky-high on her newfound feminine powers. And that first night, her so like a virgin, trembling in that black satin nightgown, when he'd felt like a trembling virgin himself when he realized what he'd unleashed.…

"Mr. Fortune?" The sea of people let him through—there wasn't anyone on the property who didn't know him. Except for the gray-haired, barrel-shaped cop who immediately stepped toward him. "I'm Detective Spaulding—Henry Spaulding."

Mac never had to say, "Find my wife. Find my baby." The detective was already reeling off what they were doing. State, city, county cops contacted. Every free man mobilized. Four cops already on foot, on the trail. Every second counted, but they had a lot going for resolving this—how fast they'd been able to move, how many witnesses had seen the man, that he was on foot. And he'd be noticeable, running with a baby.

"But just in case..." The detective started to say.

Mac already had a thousand "just in cases" threatening to erupt that volcano of fear inside him. "I want the media contacted. Show a picture of the baby. Flash it on every local news—now, while there's a chance he's still out there and people have seen him. And an appeal. He's a kidnapper. He wants money. He can have everything I've got. I just want them back safe—"

"I hear you, Mr. Fortune, but—"

He couldn't slow down. As long as he was thinking, acting, the red-hot panic couldn't erupt inside him. "I can add men to this. We've used private security services for years. Gabe Devereaux is the best—and I don't know what you need, a place to set up an information base? Pictures? Manpower? Whatever it is, I don't care, I can make it happen—"

"Mr. Fortune—"

"Don't try telling me to sit still and stay out of this," Mac said fiercely. "I can't sit. I can't wait. And I'm not the kind of average *Joe* who's going to fall apart on you. I know what a crisis is. I know how to pull people together. I can organize anything you want organized. I can get as many people here as you can use. You just have to tell me how to work with the police effort, how it's done, how you set up phone lines and everything else—''

The detective's face reflected so much empathy that Mac understood he was talking too fast, too wild. But his heart was roaring in his ears, his stomach clenched like barbed wire. He slammed a fist into his palm. "I need my wife. I need you to find her. Not tomorrow, not in an hour. Now, right now. I need to know the son of a bitch hasn't gotten her, too."

"We have no reason to think he has her—"

"That's not good enough!"

"I've got two daughters, sir. I'd be just as scared as you are. But I really want you to come inside with me and sit down. Just for a minute," the detective urged him.

"I *can't* sit. There has to be something I can do—"

"Mr. Fortune, all the things you were talking about…you're thinking good ideas, and we may do all of them. The power you've got in this city could make a difference. But right now…you have to realize it's too soon. Everyone's goal is the same—to catch this guy while the trail's hot, and there are cops on that right now. But there's been no possible time for them to report back. Once we know more about what the situation is, then we can do that organizing, do a plan. No one is going to cut you out. But the best help you can be for the next few minutes is just to take a time-out and get a grip.''

He couldn't get a grip. Because the other memory lodged in his brain like a bullet wound was the night he'd proposed to Kelly. The night she'd been attacked…in this exact same parking lot…and had come running into the building, crying for help and barreling straight into him.

Something in his blood had ignited that night. It wasn't about her being a vulnerable, pregnant woman in trouble. It wasn't about his feeling a family responsibility because of his brother's putting Kelly in a dangerous, vulnerable position. Mac had told himself those things because they were true. They were facts. They were reasons. They were nothing.

It was always her. Those killer-soft blue eyes. That silver-blond hair. The way she reached for him.

He hadn't been in love with her then. Hell, Mac didn't know what love was, then, or for a while into the marriage, either. There was always just something there, that never existed until he met her. Something in him that tugged and troubled and unsealed some rusty emotional lock that Mac hadn't even known needed a key.

Pain clawed at him. It had taken him forever to figure out he loved her more than life. But for a man who had never broken a promise, a man of honor, a man who had never failed anyone before…he'd only made one promise to Kelly.

To keep her and the baby safe.

And he'd failed her.

The April sun beat down. The detective took off; one cop car left the scene; another one drove in. People still milled around; the remaining police were going through witnesses who had seen Kelly, seen the man take off with the baby. Questions were painstakingly the same—what everyone looked like, what they were wearing—every bystander probed for any further details they might remember. Someone tried to put a foam mug of his coffee in his hand, but he didn't want it.

He couldn't remember feeling more useless, more worthless. He told himself to mentally organize all the things he could put in motion at the next stage of this, yet he couldn't seem to force himself to move. The parking lot was where Kelly and the baby had last been. These people the last ones who had seen them. He was just a husband—of no account; he hadn't seen anything, couldn't contribute anything. But they had a tie to Kel, to Annie. In his own head, he knew it was crazy, but he didn't want to leave the spot as long as anyone who had last seen Kelly and the baby were still there.

And then a cop car suddenly bounced into the lot, its light flashing but no siren on. The back passenger door opened...and there she was. Kelly, spilling out. No shoes, stockings in shreds. A navy blue dress that hugged her figure and showed off a bloody scraped knee. Her hair was all tangled, mascara tearstains shadowed her cheeks; her face was whiter than paper and there were a hundred years of terror in her eyes.

Guilt roared through him like a freight train. It was because of his failure that she looked like this, was going through this. But he corked up that shame. That was his soul problem, not hers.

He tried to reach her faster than the speed of sound. But there was an instant when her eyes darted from face to face. She spotted him, not George, not the other cops, not anyone else. And she barreled toward him as if she had that other night, as if he was the one man she really trusted that she could count on.

She was crying even before she hurled herself into his arms. "I couldn't run fast enough, Mac. I couldn't keep up and I lost him. He's got our baby. He's—"

"It's okay, it's okay..." The words were lies—Mac didn't know if anything was okay, if anything would ever be okay again. But she was shuddering and shaking from fear and shock and stress. He wrapped his arms around her, warmed her, and steered her away from prying eyes. She needed immediate care.

For the moment, that was all he could do.

Eleven

Kelly knew she was strung tight enough to snap. They'd been home for an hour now. Too long. Every second of waiting dragged out like a year of torture, but so far there was no news. The police wanted the two of them settled at home, because this was the obvious place where the kidnapper would try to contact them. Only all this inactivity of waiting felt as if she was doing nothing for Annie. She couldn't stand it.

When Mac suddenly showed in the library doorway—carrying a sloshing pan of hot water and a bottle of antiseptic—she wasn't sure whether to laugh or cry. "Aw, Mac. I can't sit. Much less sit and soak my feet. Not at a time like this!"

"Yeah, I figured you'd give me an argument." He set down the pan and a giant towel on the Oriental rug in front of the couch. Then came over to press a kiss on the top of her head. "But you can't keep pacing around on those bloody feet, Tiny. I hate to tell you this, but they're a mess.''

''I don't care about my damn feet!''

''I know you don't.'' Another kiss, intended to coax her into sitting on the couch. And when she finally plunked down, he shifted behind her, his big strong hands kneading her shoulders and the tight knots in her neck. ''There's only one thing on either of our minds. And nothing's going to get better or easier until we hear something. But those cuts and blisters aren't a joke, Kel. I know you don't want me to call a doctor—''

''No doctor,'' she said adamantly.

''And I know you're not willing to be upstairs in the tub or shower when the phone could ring—''

''No way.''

''So I'd just soak 'em for five minutes. That's all. Enough to get some disinfectant working. Okay?''

Nothing was okay. They both knew nothing was okay. But she put her bruised and blistered feet into the water, because he'd gone to the trouble of bringing it...the same way he'd brought her a hot mug of tea earlier, as thick as sludge with sugar, which he'd said she needed for shock.

Mac had been taking care of her nonstop, when she knew he was going through the same hell that she was. Except for the two policemen in the kitchen, they were alone in the house. The cops had been messing with the phone lines and setting up some kind of taping device. But now, they were just sitting and mainlining coffee and were stuck waiting for the next news, no different than she and Mac.

But it wasn't their baby who was lost. The hot tea and the disinfectant soak were no help. But Mac's warm, kneading hands on her shoulders and neck seeped some strength into her. His gentle voice and quietly taking charge and caring for her darn near broke her heart. He just kept doing things to help her get a grip.

Screaming and crying was hardly going to help. Neither was panicking. No matter what, they had to keep their heads. They had to be ready to think if the kidnapper called. They had to be smart enough, sharp enough, to respond to whatever the situation was in a way that would get Annie back to them safely.

Mac's fingers kept gently working on the impossible knots in her neck. Those knots weren't going to give, she knew. Not as long as their baby was in the hands of a stranger. But the connection she felt to Mac, his warmth, his touch, his being with her, meant everything.

"We'll get her back," she said.

"I know we will."

"It all just happened. It hasn't even been seven hours. And every cop in the city's on top of it. We'll get her back."

"I know we will." His voice was quiet and sure, exactly what she needed to hear. And then he dropped his hands from her shoulders. "Okay. Let's see those feet, Tiny."

She lifted one dripping foot, then the other. Mac winced when he hunched down and got a look at the scrapes and sores, but she wasn't paying attention. She was looking at him. His skin was gray, his eyes ancient, his face carved in austere lines of control. She understood he was holding all his fears on the inside. She understood that Mac had ways of coping that weren't like hers, but she was aware he hadn't let her be there for him. Not like the brick he was being for her.

The phone suddenly rang. The sound hit both of them like an electric shock. There were receivers all over the house, but they weren't supposed to touch any telephone until the cops had given them the okay, so they both bolted at the same time for the kitchen.

Henry Spaulding, the burly gray-haired detective, almost collided with them coming through the doorway. "We've got her!'' It was the first smile she'd seen on the man's face; she didn't know he could. "Your baby. She's okay. Perfectly okay—''

"You're *sure?*'' God, a choke welled in her throat even thicker than the tears of relief.

"Positive. I promise. She's okay.''

Mac grabbed her and hugged, his fingers tight enough to bite. "Where is she?''

"On her way. Be here in fifteen minutes,'' Henry assured them. "The kidnapper…we don't have him in custody yet, but we've got a bead. And we know who he is, Rawlin White, twenty-nine, lost a kid and a wife three years ago. Cracked up, hospitalized, got out. He was picked up last year on a complaint—a woman in a park with her baby said this guy scared her, wouldn't leave the baby alone. Another call two months ago, about him hanging around a preschool, not doing anything, just wouldn't leave. Anyway. The description was so right it rang a bell for Smythe—one of the cops, who handled the first mom's complaint. Nothing is one hundred percent until we get him, but the details all play, and so, he likely didn't plan any kidnapping, more like saw a chance to grab a baby and did. He's not dealing from a full deck, but if it'll relieve your mind any, it wasn't likely he meant to harm your baby. More like he's obsessed with the one he lost.''

"Annie—'' Mac prompted him.

"Yeah, you want to know how it went down…well, seems she started crying. Crying so loud she was drawing attention. Panicked him. He put her down and ran. Like I said, we haven't got him yet. But a woman called from an office building, the one who saw him, saw him put down the baby. She's a grandma herself, called 911, took the baby into her office until the officers got there…''

There was more, but Kelly just couldn't listen any longer. She was waiting, waiting, at the open front door when the police car pulled in. Before the woman police officer carrying the baby even stepped out, Kelly was hurling herself toward the car. Annie was crying. Furious, hungry cries. Furious, hungry, healthy cries. Nothing had ever sounded so good in her entire life.

She grabbed Annie and clutched; Mac came up right beside her and clutched the two of them the same way. His eyes welled with tears no different than her own.

By midnight, the excitement was over, the house quiet again, yet Mac couldn't seem to settle down. Neither could she. Both were stress-tired beyond any capacity to think, yet they found themselves standing in front of the crib, watching Annie sleep.

"We have to go to bed, Mac. This is silly. She's fine. We're both exhausted."

"I know. But..."

But neither of them could seem to stop looking at the baby. Kelly couldn't stop thinking how lucky they'd been, how different this day could have ended. Yet Annie really seemed none the worse for wear. She wasn't bruised or hurt, just initially furiously hungry. She'd splashed through her bath just like any other day. Squawked when she and Mac tried to grab a bite. Accepted in true-princess fashion that her parents were going to hold her ceaselessly until night had long fallen, but eventually she'd dropped off so solidly that it was crazy not to put her in her crib.

Kelly knew her vision was blurring from tiredness, yet still couldn't stop looking. Savoring the baby's rosebud mouth that was stuffed with a thumb. Her diapered bottom in the air. Her eyelashes like pale feathers on her pink cheeks.

Mac was quiet. He'd barely said anything since the cops had left and they had Annie alone. But now he touched her shoulder. "Come on, you," he said gently. "You really do need to get off your feet. Those blisters and cuts aren't going to heal with you walking around.''

She knew he was right. They both stumbled into his bedroom, peeled off their clothes and then sank into Mac's bed with a matched pair of exhausted sighs. Instinctively she rolled into his arms. ''We're all right, Mac.''

''Yes.''

''She's safe.''

''Yes.''

''We're safe. It's over. It was horrible, but it's over.''

She snuggled closer. Making love was the last thought in her head; she couldn't remember being more exhausted, and knew Mac was, too. But what they'd been through was still pounding in her head. She snuggled a leg between his, her arms wrapping around his back. She felt his body becoming aroused, but she just needed to touch him. To be with him. To affirm life, what their family of three had survived this day, what they'd shared. When she tipped her head, his mouth was there, waiting to offer a kiss that was both soft and fierce and echoed all the emotions pulsing through her.

But then Mac shifted. He kissed her brow, smoothed back her hair and turned on his back.

She didn't think anything of his turning away. Not that night, nor the next. They'd been through an agonizing ordeal. Recovering just couldn't be an instantaneous thing.

But when another week passed, Kelly slowly realized that Mac had turned ultraquiet from the minute the baby had been returned to them. He answered questions. He handled family and business and media questions following the incident. And he handled the baby no differently than he always did. But he wasn't the same with her. They'd slept side by side all these nights without making love, and he hadn't volunteered a word of conversation that wasn't required. The shadows under his eyes told tales about his restless nights.

The obvious finally occurred to her. Mac could be blaming her for the kidnapping. God knew, she could understand that, because she'd been blaming herself.

* * *

The following Tuesday was a balmy-warm spring day, and when Annie woke from her afternoon nap, Kelly told Benz and Martha that she was going to take the baby for a short outing. They had a fit and a half about her going anywhere alone, but Kelly explained that was exactly the reason. She hadn't left the place in a week; it was time to take the plunge. It was too beautiful a day not to enjoy it with Annie, and all she planned to do was drive to her old apartment and pick up her summer clothes. They'd be within reach of a phone and she didn't expect to be gone more than an hour.

Those things were true. But she also hoped that a little escape away from home might help her think more clearly. Within minutes, she was parked in the quiet neighborhood, had Annie secured in a front pack and was climbing the stairs to her old apartment. The place smelled stuffy and closed-up when she first walked in. She threw open some windows and then just wandered around.

She remembered how much she'd first loved the apartment, but now it only felt alien and unfamiliar. Somehow Mac's things had become hers, and hers part of his. The place had once been a joyful symbol of her independence and pride in being able to cope on her own...but it seemed as if she'd been a girl when she lived here, those joys minor compared to the richness of a relationship she'd been building with Mac. Or thought she'd been building.

Kelly sighed, and automatically stroked Annie's soft head. "This isn't working too well, lovebug. We might as well pick up those summer clothes and get out of here."

She'd just started emptying out the bedroom closet when she heard a rap on the door, immediately followed by Mac's voice. "Kelly, don't be scared—it's just me."

Mac had a key, of course, but she'd just never expected to hear his voice. His speaking up swiftly was so typically considerate—he knew she'd be fearful of strangers right now—and she hustled toward the door, her first response simply a delighted surprised smile that he was here. Mac met her halfway in the hall, dressed still for work in a gray striped suit and formal white shirt. Her smile quickly faded when she saw his grave expression.

"You're leaving me."

She thought she'd heard him wrong. He'd blurted out the comment so suddenly, out of nowhere. *"What?"*

Faster than he could clench his jaw, he side-roaded down a different conversational path. "I just happened to call home and got Martha. She said you'd come over here..."

"Yeah. When it hit seventy this afternoon, I realized I didn't have anything cooler to wear than jeans. My summer clothes were still here. I just figured it was a good time to pick them up." She hesitated. "More to the truth, I just needed to get out."

"Yeah, I can understand that."

Maybe he could. But she'd seen something stark and sharp flash in his eyes, as if she'd said something to hurt him. So she tried to explain further. "I was doing the princess in the tower routine, Mac. Yesterday, I even asked Martha to hit a quick stop when we ran out of milk, rather than going myself. I just thought, enough was enough. I knew I was scared. But I could see myself falling into this pattern, just stay home, stay safe." She shook her head. "It's not that I needed to go anywhere. I just wanted to prove to myself that I could."

"It's twice you've had to deal with that kind of fear in the last few months."

She nodded. "I admit, it'll probably be a while before I stop feeling skittery near crowds—unless I'm with you. But coming here was easy, just a short drive, no danger, no strangers..." Her voice trailed off. All these lubbering explanations were a waste of time, when there was only one thing on her mind. "Mac, I have no idea what you meant. You thought I was coming back to my old apartment...to stay? Without you?"

His mouth opened to answer her, but then he just seemed to swallow and dam up. Naturally Annie chose that moment to start fussing—probably because it was close to her late-afternoon nursing time. Kelly said quietly, firmly, "I don't really need to do anything here today. Let's just all go home. But after we put the baby to bed—Mac, we're going to talk about this."

"I think we'd better," he agreed.

A thousand things roiled in her mind over the next few hours. She'd been blaming herself nonstop for the kidnapping attempt—for not being careful enough, for not unlocking the car doors before Annie was in her arms, for not getting the guard before she'd stepped out of the car. But if Mac were blaming her, he'd never said a critical word...nor would there seem any logical connection to his suddenly thinking she was leaving him.

So something else had to be wrong, and the same old fears sprang into her mind like weeds. Maybe the kidnapping had brought some festering feelings to the surface, made Mac believe this marriage just wasn't working out. He'd never really wanted her, never *chosen* her. They'd been through things that brought them close, but that wasn't the same as being crazy in love. Mac had been trapped into this marriage because of his sense of honor. His feeling responsible.

Almost as soon as they were home, Annie picked up on her anxiety and started a whining cry. She nursed her, and then she and Mac rocked the baby in rotating turns. They ate dinner in shifts. She showered and changed into a fresh sweatshirt and jeans while Mac paced with Annie in the Great room. He showered and shed his suit for an old pair of black sweats while she paced with Annie in the library. But when it was finally baby-bedtime, Annie promptly settled into a deep snooze like an angel…possibly because she sensed her mom had had a total change of mood.

Kelly wasn't precisely calm, but she'd had hours to think—and specifically she'd been thinking about her husband's unique and unquenchable sense of honor. It was always a key to the man she loved. She'd made a mistake, forgetting that, and the minute the baby fell asleep, she went searching for Mac. The open French doors clued her in that he was outside on the patio overlooking the woods. She grabbed his jacket to pull over her shoulders and stepped out.

The sun had just set, a blush of color still staining the cheeks of the horizon, but the sky was fast turning a midnight blue and the air turning crisp. She heard a hoot owl's mournful cry in the woods, saw a graceful doe and her yearling grazing on the far knoll. But all she really noticed was Mac, standing still and silent, his shoulders as stiff as if he were bracing for a blow.

The last thing she wanted was to deliver a blow, but she did want to make him think. So she took a breath for courage, and then spoke up loud and clear. "If you want a divorce, Mac, you can forget it. I don't care about all those silly papers we signed. I'm not leaving you."

He spun around. Even in the gathering shadows, she saw his bleak dark eyes. In the beginning she hadn't understood that his most austere look of control masked a heart-deep vulnerability. But she did now. His loneliness had always come from a need to do the right thing, even when that cost him. She just wished she'd remembered that through this long week, when he'd been withdrawing from her.

"You think *I* want a divorce?"

The shock in his voice gave her courage another boost. She stomped closer. "Well, in your shoes, I sure would. And I've thought about that plenty. Your being trapped into marrying a stranger. A pregnant woman yet, who turned your whole life upside down. If I were an honorable woman, I'd admit you did the right thing, but now that part's over and you should be able to get out, if that's what you want. But I don't seem to have your sense of honor—"

Mac was shaking his head in total confusion. "Kel, you have this all wrong. I never once—"

But she wasn't about to let him get a word in until she'd gotten some critical things said. "Forget honor. From my shoes, I'd have to be crazy to let you go—and frankly, my attitude is entirely your fault. The problem is, you've loved me every way a man can love a woman. You've been there for me, over and over. Through my crazy pregnancy mood swings, through labor, through times I was scared. You made your house, my house. And God knows, you opened up my world in your bed. And all for a woman you were stuck with."

"I never felt stuck with you, Tiny."

That "Tiny" echoed in her heart like bells. His guard was going down if he were calling her Tiny. And she could see some of that tension easing out of his shoulders. But not all. "Sure you did. And you were. Stuck being responsible for me all the time—why, I'm guessing you even felt responsible for the kidnapping thing, didn't you?"

The way his eyes flashed black in the shadows, she knew she'd hit bone. And suddenly, out came the pain, his voice rusty and hoarse with it. "You married me to keep you safe, Kelly. It was having a Fortune baby that put you at risk—twice now. And I promised to protect you. And I can't stop feeling like I failed you in the worst way.''

She felt his hurt as if someone had stabbed her instead of him. ''Oh, Mac. That's why you thought I was leaving you? But you have this so wrong. You never failed me in anything.'' There was nothing she wanted more than to reach out and grab him. Hold him. Love him. Make that harsh expression disappear from his face. But she had to convince him that she meant that love, first.

''I spent a week beating myself up over the kidnapping,'' she said quietly. ''And I should have known—you were doing it to yourself even worse. But I've gone over and over how that happened, and the truth is…this wasn't about either of us not being careful enough. It wasn't about *us*. It was about an emotionally unstable man who happened to be walking through a parking lot at that moment in time. Now how could anyone be protected against something like that?''

''Maybe not. But in the beginning, I seemed to have arrogantly assumed that the Fortune name would help solve problems for you. Instead all I can see is that it put you at further risk.''

''You and I do have risks that maybe most couples don't have.'' She wasn't going to pretend otherwise. ''Your name comes with some special problems. You've got way too many people calling you Mr. Fortune. Way too many people counting on you night and day. And it doesn't help that you've got a sense of honor bigger than the sky. But you're the one who gave me the answer to that a long time ago.''

''I did?''

She nodded. ''You're the one who said it—that we had the freedom to make a relationship our own way. By our own rules. And I think that means that we protect each other, but that has to be a two-way street, Mac. I don't want to be another responsibility for you. When I'm scared,

I want your arms around me. But when you're scared, I need to know that you can tell me. And that you know I'll be there for you.''

She waited. Unsure if he really heard her. Unsure if she had anything else she could try saying that might get through to him. But then his voice came through the velvet gray dusk like the stroke of a caress.

''Kel?''

''What?''

He said quietly, ''I was scared. Scared soulless. That you wanted to leave me.''

In two seconds flat she was in his arms. He took her mouth in a fierce, crushing kiss that laid bare the kind of vulnerability that only a strong man could have. Oh, she had work to do with him. Mac was never going to stop trying to do the right thing. She'd never believed she was a strong enough woman for him, but loving him had taught him that there was a man's kind of strength. And a woman's. She kissed him back, pouring her heart into warming him, loving him, being there for him. ''I was never leaving you,'' she whispered. ''I couldn't possibly love you more, Mac.''

''And I love you. You're the wonder in my heart, Kel.'' His fingers touched her cheek, her hair. And then his lips dipped down for another kiss, this one softer, slower, as if he were tasting the future, and sharing promises about what he wanted for her, for them. ''There are a couple of questions I've wanted to ask you for some time.''

''Now?'' She could have sworn they were through talking.

''Now. They won't take long.'' But he took a breath, and then said slowly, ''Would you be my bride, Kelly Sinclair? Would you let me promise to love and honor and cherish you? To be the father of your children? To love you all the days of my life?''

"Holy kamoly, Mac. You're going to make me cry." Her eyes were already blurring with silvery tears. "I could have sworn we already did that."

"Yeah. But I'm thinking we should do it again. This time, just for us. And I was thinking we could do another ceremony on New Year's Eve, because that was a heck of a symbolic way to start last year. But then I thought..."

She had no trouble finishing his sentence. "Why wait? You and I alone make the rules for us. And there's no reason on earth we can't start a brand-new year right now."

He kissed her again. "I like that idea far more, love."

So did she. She saw the smile glowing in his eyes—the one with the touch of wicked that always ignited her blood. But it was the love in his expression that fired her blood far more. The cool-spiced night seemed to have miraculously heated up. She noticed his sweatshirt pulled off with remarkable ease. And her sweatshirt disappeared even faster than magic. But it wasn't magic that had made their marriage real, she thought, but the power of love and wonder they'd found in each other.

* * * * *

Want to find out what happens to Renee Riley?
Look for Renee and Garrett Fortune's love story in

Society Bride

by

Elizabeth Bevarly

coming to Silhouette Desire's Fortune's Children:
The Brides miniseries
in February.

And now for a sneak preview of
Society Bride, *please turn the page.*

———

"You know...you've been following your heart all this time, and where has it gotten you?"

Renee Riley bit her lower lip and didn't answer. Mainly because she had no answer to give. Her father was right. She had followed her heart, and her heart had left her unemployed, with no prospects on the horizon. Still, it was her personal happiness at stake, she reminded herself. Then again, was she really happy?

Before she could offer herself an answer, her father piped up to give his own take on matters. "Now, if you marry Lyle Norton, then Riley Communications would remain a family-owned business. It would be there in the future for *your* children—in case one of my grandchildren wanted to go into a business begun by a family member generations ago. I'm only trying to preserve what's ours, honey. I'm this close to losing our legacy, Renee. But if you marry Lyle, it will preserve an entire way of life for all the Rileys to come."

A legacy, Renee repeated to herself. Great. Suddenly she was the sole keeper of a family tradition.

Renee sighed fitfully as she ran her hand through her hair. It had been a long day, and she was too tired from all the festivities. So quietly, reluctantly, she said, "Okay, Daddy. I'll think about marrying Lyle."

And she would, too, she promised herself as her father kissed her on the cheek and made his way back into the crowd of celebratory guests at her friend Kelly's wedding. But just not here. Not where there was so much warmth and promise.

Confident she could steal a few minutes without being missed, she eased out of the conference room door. Everyone was too caught up in the celebration going on inside to notice the disappearance of one little, nerve-racked maid of honor.

For a long time, she simply sat in Kelly's office, gazing out the window at the snow. Renee thought about a lot of things. But mostly, Renee thought about love.

Growing restless, she donned her coat and headed for the small terrace at the end of the corridor.

Someone else *was* outside, however, she discovered the moment she stepped onto the terrace. A tall, dark figure leaned against the bricks not ten feet away from her, one knee bent with his foot braced against the wall behind him. His head was tipped back, and he was staring up at the sky, but he didn't seem to be seeing much of anything.

"Hi," she heard herself say before she even realized she had intended to speak.

The man stared at her greeting, snapping his head around to look at her.

Strange, Renee thought. Somehow, though, she didn't feel the least bit threatened. On the contrary, Renee sensed a wall of defense surrounding the guy that was unmistakable.

"Hi, yourself," he replied. His voice was deep, smooth, warm, reminding Renee of a generous shot of cognac—good, old cognac, the kind that went down oh, so smoothly and gradually heated you up from the inside out.

As she drew nearer, Renee noticed that he was an exceedingly handsome man. His eyes were dark, and his mouth... His mouth was at once soft and fierce, inviting and wary, luscious and forbidding. Much like the man, she couldn't help but think.

"I'm a friend of the bride's. Renee Riley," she said, clutching her coat tightly around her.

"The maid of honor," he said.

She smiled. "You noticed?"

"Oh, yeah. I noticed. Garrett Fortune. Cousin of the groom," he added, folding his fingers confidently over hers, completely eclipsing her own hand.

"So...what did you think of the wedding?"

"I thought the wedding was beautiful," he said amiably. "And I also think marriage is a complete waste of time and a total farce," he added in much the same tone of voice.

"Maybe not having love in their relationship will make Kelly and Mac's union stronger."

He narrowed his eyes at her. "Funny," he said softly, "but somehow, I had you pegged as the more romantic type. Hearts and flowers and love forever-after. All that mushy stuff."

"Yeah, well, maybe there *are* better reasons for getting married. Maybe it's *commitment* that's what's really important in marriage, you know? Not love, not passion, but...responsibility. Obligation."

"Gee, keeping saying it over and over like that, and maybe eventually you'll start to believe it."

Below them, the city erupted in celebration. Car horns blared, people shouted, and faintly, the soft strains of *Auld Lang Syne* crept up through the stillness of the cold night air.

"It must be midnight," he said, extending his glass toward her in a silent offer. "Happy New Year, Renee."

"Happy New Year, Garrett."

And then, he suddenly dipped his head down and kissed her. Just like that. And instead of pulling away, Garrett took a step toward her, circling one arm around Renee's waist to draw her closer still.

But she didn't push him away.

Garrett lowered his head again, to kiss her once more. But just when his mouth settled possessively over hers, Renee turned her head and gently pushed him away.

"I have to go," she said hastily, avoiding his eyes. "My father's waiting."

As new years went, this one wasn't starting off well at all.

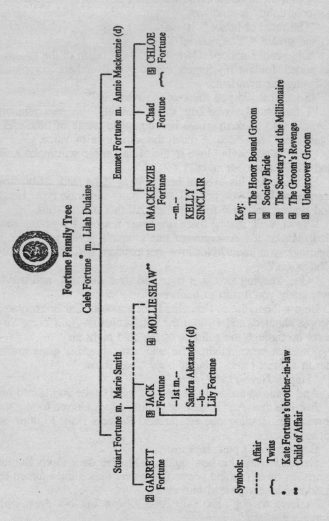

Fortune Family Tree

Caleb Fortune* m. Lilah Dulaine

Stuart Fortune m. Marie Smith

Emmet Fortune m. Annie Mackenzie (d)

② GARRETT Fortune

③ JACK Fortune

④ MOLLIE SHAW**

① MACKENZIE Fortune

Chad Fortune

⑤ CHLOE Fortune

--1st m.--
Sandra Alexander (d)
--j--
Lily Fortune

--m.--
KELLY SINCLAIR

Key:
① The Honor Bound Groom
② Society Bride
③ The Secretary and the Millionaire
④ The Groom's Revenge
⑤ Undercover Groom

Symbols:
--- Affair
{ Twins
. Kate Fortune's brother-in-law
•• Child of Affair

If you enjoyed what you just read,
then we've got an offer you can't resist!

Take 2 bestselling love stories FREE!
Plus get a FREE surprise gift!

Clip this page and mail it to Silhouette Reader Service™

IN U.S.A.
3010 Walden Ave.
P.O. Box 1867
Buffalo, N.Y. 14240-1867

IN CANADA
P.O. Box 609
Fort Erie, Ontario
L2A 5X3

YES! Please send me 2 free Silhouette Desire® novels and my free surprise gift. Then send me 6 brand-new novels every month, which I will receive months before they're available in stores. In the U.S.A., bill me at the bargain price of $3.12 plus 25¢ delivery per book and applicable sales tax, if any*. In Canada, bill me at the bargain price of $3.49 plus 25¢ delivery per book and applicable taxes**. That's the complete price and a savings of over 10% off the cover prices—what a great deal! I understand that accepting the 2 free books and gift places me under no obligation ever to buy any books. I can always return a shipment and cancel at any time. Even if I never buy another book from Silhouette, the 2 free books and gift are mine to keep forever. So why not take us up on our invitation. You'll be glad you did!

225 SEN CNFA
326 SEN CNFC

Name	(PLEASE PRINT)	
Address	Apt.#	
City	State/Prov.	Zip/Postal Code

* Terms and prices subject to change without notice. Sales tax applicable in N.Y.
** Canadian residents will be charged applicable provincial taxes and GST.
All orders subject to approval. Offer limited to one per household.
® are registered trademarks of Harlequin Enterprises Limited.

DES99   ©1998 Harlequin Enterprises Limited

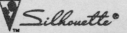

SILHOUETTE® *Desire®*

COMING NEXT MONTH

#1195 A KNIGHT IN RUSTY ARMOR—Dixie Browning
Man of the Month/The Lawless Heirs
When Travis Holiday found out he had a son, he realized it was time to settle down—no more heroics! Then a long-haired goddess named Ruanna Roberts was stranded in a storm, and Travis just had to save her. But Ruanna was determined to rescue *Travis!* Could she crumble the armor around his soul and claim his heart for her own…?

#1196 SOCIETY BRIDE—Elizabeth Bevarly
Fortune's Children: The Brides
Weeks away from a business marriage and Rene Riley was secluded on a remote ranch with the man of her dreams! Though cowboy Garrett Fortune defined unbridled passion, Rene was the only woman he wanted. He just had to convince her that the only *partnership* she was going to enter into was a marriage to him!

#1197 DEDICATED TO DEIRDRE—Anne Marie Winston
Butler County Brides
Ronan Sullivan and Deirdre Patten hadn't seen one another for years, but one look and Deirdre knew the desire was still there. Ronan needed a place to stay, and Deirdre had a room to rent. But opening her home—and heart—to Ronan could prove very perilous indeed.…

#1198 THE OUTLAW JESSE JAMES—Cindy Gerard
Outlaw Hearts
Rodeo was the only mistress in cowboy Jesse James's life. He liked slow, hot seductions and short, fast goodbyes. Then Sloan Gantry sashayed into his life. Could this sweet temptress convince the "outlaw" that the only place to run was straight into her arms…?

#1199 SECRET DAD—Raye Morgan
Single mom Charlie Smith would do anything for her child—even marry rugged mercenary Denver McCaine. She now had his protection, but Charlie was wondering how much tender affection one woman could take before dreams of happily-ever-after took hold of her wistful heart.…

#1200 LITTLE MISS INNOCENT?—Lori Foster
No matter what he did, Dr. Daniel Sawyer could not shake his desire for Lace McGee. The sweet seductress had a tempting mouth and a will of iron. But there was also uncertainty in Lace's eyes. Was it there to drive him away—or did she hide an innocence he had never suspected?